For Leo —

May your spirit
always ROAR
With Love + Eternal Light
Caroline

The Oaken Door

The Lion of Wales Series:
Cold My Heart
The Oaken Door
Of Men and Dragons

The Gareth and Gwen Medieval Mysteries

The Bard's Daughter
The Good Knight
The Uninvited Guest
The Fourth Horseman
The Fallen Princess
The Unlikely Spy
The Lost Brother

The After Cilmeri Series:

Daughter of Time
Footsteps in Time
Winds of Time
Prince of Time
Crossroads in Time
Children of Time
Exiles in Time
Castaways in Time
Ashes of Time
Warden of Time

The Last Pendragon Saga

The Last Pendragon
The Pendragon's Quest

www.sarahwoodbury.com

Book Two in the *Lion of Wales* Series

The
OAKEN
DOOR

by

SARAH WOODBURY

The Oaken Door
Copyright © 2015 by Sarah Woodbury

This is a work of fiction.

To Gareth

A Brief Guide to Welsh Names and Places

Aberystwyth –Ah-bare-IH-stwith

Bedwyr – BED-weer

Bwlch y Ddeufaen – Boolk ah THEY-vine (the 'th' is soft as in 'forth')

Cadfael – CAD-file

Cadwallon – Cad-WASH-lon

Caernarfon – ('ae' makes a long i sound like in 'kite') Kire-NAR-von

Dafydd – DAH-vith

Dolwyddelan – dole-with-EH-lan (the 'th' is soft as in 'forth')

Gawain – GAH-wine

Geraint – GER-ighnt

Gruffydd – GRIFF-ith

Gwalchmai – GWALK-my ('ai' makes a long i sound like in 'kite')

Gwenllian – Gwen-SHLEE-an

Gwladys – Goo-LAD-iss

Gwynedd – GWIN-eth

Huw – Hugh

Hywel – H'wel

Ieuan – ieu sounds like the cheer, 'yay' so YAY-an

Llywelyn – shlew-ELL-in

Meilyr – MY-lir

Myrddin – MER-thin

Owain – OH-wine

Rhuddlan – RITH-lan

Rhun – Rin

Rhys – Reese

Sion – Shawn

Tudur – TIH-deer

Usk – Isk

Cast of Characters

The Welsh

King Arthur ap Uther (born 480 AD)
Ambrosius—King of Wales (deceased 501 AD), uncle to Arthur
Myrddin—Knight (born 501 AD)
Nell—Myrddin's friend (born 507 AD)
Ifan—Myrddin's friend

Geraint—Knight
Gawain—Knight, Gareth's brother
Gareth—Knight, Gawain's brother
Bedwyr—Knight, Arthur's seneschal
Cai—Arthur's half-brother
Dafydd—Archbishop of Wales

The Saxons

Modred—Arthur's nephew (b. 497 AD)
Cedric—Lord of Brecon
Edgar—Arthur's nephew, Lord of Wigmore
Agravaine—Lord of Oswestry
Wulfere—Modred's captain

1

8 November 537 AD

"*Myrddin! Get over here!*"

I obeyed, riding toward Gawain, my captain. At his grim look, I pulled up beside him, reaching for my sword— not to fight him, but because he already held his.

"*The Saxons are here!*" *he said.*

I squinted in the direction he pointed, but could see nothing beyond movement in the branches opposite. "I'll root them out, my lord."

I gathered my men together and we crossed the creek to the north of the church where King Arthur waited even now to meet with Lord Edgar. I knew it was a trap. It was always a trap. I struggled to turn aside but we rode relentlessly on, across the creek, up the bank, and through the trees. Once we left the protection of the woods, the arrows flew and Ifan shouted that we must turn back.

"Myrddin! No!" As I charged the Saxon line, a woman screamed. The screaming grew louder but I ignored it, instead spurring my horse forward, my heart racing. "Myrddin!"

N ell sat up with a start, her breath coming in gasps. She could still see the dream, hanging before her eyes like a veil, even as Myrddin sprang from his pallet and came towards her through it.

"What is it?"

"Just a dream." Nell put a hand to her chest in hopes that it would ease her racing heart.

"Of St. Asaph?" Myrddin crouched before her.

Nell took in a breath and let it out. "No." She lifted a hand to him and he took it, warming it in his two larger ones. "Not that. It was one I often have. It's nothing."

"Is it?" Myrddin said.

Nell froze, hearing the change of tone in his voice, and looked into his face. She'd asked that he leave a candle burning in its dish and it still guttered, within moments of going out but still giving off enough light to show his expression. "Yes. Why?"

"You called my name," he said. "Or rather, cried it."

"Oh."

"I'm curious that if it was a dream you've often had, that you would have dreamt of me before you met me."

Nell twitched her shoulders. For so many years she'd longed to tell someone of the dream, but now that it came to it, she couldn't. He would think her—no, know her—crazed. She gazed into Myrddin's face, warring with herself, unable to answer. "It—" She stopped. "I didn't—"

Myrddin sat back on his heels. "It's all right. You don't have to tell me right now if you don't want to."

Nell didn't know if that was really better or not. If not for the screaming, he'd probably have thought she was dreaming of him in a romantic way but was too embarrassed to admit it. It irked her how wrong that was but had no way to fix it. Under his gaze, she forced herself to relax and lie down. But she didn't turn her back to him as she had earlier. Instead, she studied him as he was studying her.

He'd made sure, once she'd found space for them in one of the small, closet-like sleeping rooms in the manor house, that this was truly what she wanted. The room had been empty as they'd entered. He'd closed the door to lean against it while she shifted one of the pallets so it no longer abutted any of the others.

"After this, there's no going back, Nell," he'd said.

Nell had laughed, the sound coming more harshly than she'd intended. "It's not very nun-like is it?" She arrested her movements to focus on him. "It's better this way, Myrddin. I slept that first night amongst the other women, ten of us strewn across the floor. My dreaming woke them three times. They don't want me there and I don't want to lie among them."

"I'm not saying it's uncommon," Myrddin said. "It's done all the time. Most of the men here haven't married their women, but none of those women spent the last ten years in a convent. This is going to ruin your reputation."

"Or yours?" She looked up at him, truly worried about the arrangement for the first time. "The king—"

"Couldn't care less," he said. "His concern, like mine, would be for you."

"This is my choice."

"If you say so." He gestured to a spot against the opposite wall from where she sat. "I gather my pallet is over there."

"You gather correctly." She shot him a grin. "If another woman catches your eye, just tell me and I'll make myself scarce."

"Damn it, Nell. " He'd turned on her, his hands on his hips. "This isn't funny."

"Isn't it?" she said. "I have to look at it this way. Otherwise, the only other choice is despair."

Now, Myrddin invoked that earlier conversation. "I know about despair, Nell." He eased backwards onto his pallet. "I didn't realize it at the time, but last night when you spoke to me of it, you weren't speaking just about what happened at St. Asaph, or even Llanfaes, were you?"

"No," Nell said. "Despair is a companion with whom I'm long acquainted."

Myrddin matched her, lying on his side with the blankets pulled to his chin. "I have dreams too, Nell."

Nell nodded, but still wasn't ready to reveal her true thoughts: *Not like mine, you don't.*

* * * * *

Myrddin slept past the dawn and awoke, his brain churning, thinking about Nell, knowing that she'd dreamt of him even if she wouldn't admit it. He hoped the dream was a good one but somehow doubted it.

Nell's auburn hair cascaded off the edge of the pallet, having come loose from her braid in the restless night. She turned her head, met his eyes, looked away, and then looked back. "Thank you for understanding."

Myrddin sat up. "I didn't say I understood," he said. "I just decided not to press you right away. At some point soon, I'm going to ask you to tell me what is going on behind that sweet smile."

"Oh, is that it?" she said, giving him the smile he wanted. "Well, not this moment anyway." She got to her feet. "While you wait, you can help me dress."

Myrddin took that for what it was—a chaste invitation. Well-bred women wore elaborate skirts that scraped the ground, got in the way, and forced women to walk in a mincing fashion. At Arthur's insistence, Nell had given away both the homespun dress which the men had ripped at St. Asaph before Myrddin had rescued her and the coarse dress from Caerhun that blood-stains had irreparably damaged. In exchange, she now wore the fashionable gown of a lady, which was a bit harder to get into.

By the time they arrived in the great hall, it was full of people and rumors. A rider from Modred had arrived and the inhabitants of Garth Celyn were abuzz with what the letter he carried contained. Myrddin pulled Nell to a seat near Ifan, who (after a knowing look that encompassed them both and what he assumed had gone on between them in the night) shrugged when Myrddin queried him.

"Your guess is as good as mine," Ifan said. "Lord Aelric carried a letter from King Arthur to Modred; I assume this is Modred's response. It won't change anything."

"But with the battle at the Strait—" Nell said.

Myrddin shook his head. "Modred won't even mention it. He believes he has the better of King Arthur; such is his arrogance that he believes it is our king who is in rebellion and in danger of excommunication. By his lights, our only recourse is to beg for mercy."

"Bollocks to that," Ifan said.

Myrddin caught Nell's eye. "What do you think Archbishop Dafydd has told him?" she said.

"It's what Modred has promised the Church, more like," Ifan said, the same sour expression on his face.

Before they'd finished their breakfast, Gareth appeared at the table. He put his hands flat on the wood and leaned heavily on them, the weight of the world on his back. "The king wants you." He looked directly at Myrddin.

Nell, who wasn't invited, wrinkled her nose in annoyance. Myrddin shrugged back at her and got to his feet. He followed Gareth to the rear of the hall and down the corridor to Arthur's receiving room near one of the towers. In the room already were King Arthur, Lord Cai, his face a thundercloud, Geraint, and Bedwyr. The figure of Cai drew Myrddin's attention and his eyes narrowed.

Myrddin hated the man—all the more after the exchange from the day before. Nell, in her former life as a nun, would have told him that it was wrong to hate at all, but when speaking of Cai, anything less than hatred would have been doing him a disservice. The man begged for retribution, but to his regret, Myrddin would never be the one to give it.

Over the years, Cai had betrayed his brother in many ways and by diverse means, even to the point of conspiring with Modred to wage war against Arthur (twice), and an assassination attempt. Whenever Myrddin was in Cai's presence, he avoided looking at him at all and worked very hard not to show his disdain. Arthur's face didn't reveal what he thought of Cai either, but then, he'd spent a lifetime masking his feelings towards his brother. Most of the time, it was best not to think on it, especially since Cai stood beside Arthur once again.

Myrddin had arrived in the middle of a conversation between Cai and Arthur, and this time they were in agreement, even if both were angry. Arthur stood, his back to the other men in the room, staring out at the heavily falling rain which was making muddy puddles in the courtyard.

Cai, for his part, snorted his derision, disgust in every line of his body. "At least he offers you a plot of land in Mercia in exchange for Eryri. Modred's letter to me states that 'peace' means I must take the cross, travel to the holy land, and never return to Wales. I'll give him peace! He is a fool."

Arthur turned to his brother, his expression mild. "If we deny his requests, he will see to it that the Archbishop excommunicates us. He states his intention boldly."

"Archbishops have not always spoken for God to our kings." Cai spat out his response. "If we are excommunicate for protecting our country and our people, then so be it."

The stance was a brave one and for the first time in his life, Myrddin found himself agreeing with Cai. He had more fire behind his words since he'd started this war. It almost made Myrddin think that he had concern for something or someone besides himself.

"And these messengers bother me," King Arthur said. "They bear a white flag of truce, but they wear Agravaine's colors, not Modred's."

At the mention of Agravaine, every man in the room hissed under his breath. Everywhere Arthur had turned of late, there Agravaine had been. He was the key coordinator of military activity in Wales for Modred. He'd gained this position over the heads of all the other barons who supported him, including Lord Edgar of Powys and Lord Cedric of Brecon, Modred's cousins.

"These riders will do what they can to spy on us," Bedwyr said. "We don't want them running around Eryri unobserved."

"That's what I need you for, Myrddin." King Arthur had finally noted him in his corner. "Follow them as far as the Conwy River and then return to me this evening. Take Ifan. When I'm ready, you will carry my answer to Modred."

"Yes, my lord," Myrddin said.

"Take Deiniol with you as well." Cai halted Myrddin's progress towards the door. "He's your brother, I believe."

His stomach roiling, Myrddin inwardly corrected him: *foster brother*. "Yes, my lord," he said instead, and turned away.

Did he know how much Myrddin hated him? *He* being Cai, and *him* being Deiniol, who knew damn well that Myrddin despised him down to his ugly boots.

"What's wrong?" Nell caught Myrddin as he walked stiff-legged across the hall, heading towards the front doors, which opened as another soldier left the room, exposing the hall to the elements.

It was cold, even for November. A dozen men and horses were preparing to ride on similar missions—to other lords and barons whose estates were within a few days' ride of Garth Celyn. Modred had sent a letter to the Council of Wales, as well as one each to Cai and Arthur. The Council needed to see it, discuss it, and respond, just as Arthur and Cai did. Raindrops reflected off the links of the men's mail which were just visible beneath the thick wool of their cloaks. Myrddin didn't envy them even as he acknowledged that he would soon be one of them.

"I'm sent to follow the Saxon riders who brought the messages to the king," Myrddin said. "To make sure they return to their side of the Conwy."

"And that makes you angry?"

Myrddin halted and turned to her, forcing down the anger and the memories that had formed a film over his eyes.

The rain drips down my neck into the collar of my linen shirt. Ripped and torn after my struggles in the woods over the last hour, it provides little protection anyway. If I ever reach the safety of the castle, I will leave it in the rag pile on my way in.

I shiver. "Come on, Myrddin, you spineless bastard," I say. "Move!"

But I cannot. I bend aside a branch of the bush in which I'm cowering and peer though the murk, looking for my pursuer. I see nothing but the rain and the muddy track separating me from the gatehouse of the castle.

Bracing myself, I leave the safety of my bush. In ten quick steps, I'm through the gatehouse and cross the bailey at a run, heading for the stables. I reach it and then press my back against the wall beside the open doorway. I listen for movement, to calm myself and become one with my surrounding as I've been taught, but my beating heart and the pounding rain overwhelm my senses.

At last, I risk entry. I slip through the doorway and head for the shadow of the horse stalls. A horse whickers a gentle greeting and I touch his nose to quiet him. From the door at the far end of the stables, it's a dozen yards to a side door of the keep. Once there, I'll be safe. For now. I reach the last stall and quicken my pace, sensing freedom. Instead, the door swings open and I'm face to face with Deiniol. He grins.

I back away.

A single lantern lights the expansive space between the doorway and the horses. The light glints off a knife Deiniol holds. He shifts it from one hand to the other as I watch. Deiniol is a seasoned fighter, full grown and strong. Even though I'm already sixteen, I'm still a scrawny half-child, speaking in a voice that breaks instead of the low voice of a man.

Deiniol has always been bigger than I, possessing a cruel streak I'd discovered before I could talk. There are more ways to hurt than through physical pain and Deiniol has tried them all on me at one time or another. He's hounded me all afternoon and it's as if this moment is the culmination of a lifetime of animosity. I'll have one chance to escape him, if I've any chance at all.

Between one second and the next, Deiniol moves forward and I spring to my right, only to find myself caught between two large hands that grip my arms and twist them behind my back. A booted foot comes around my legs and pinions them. I twist and jerk my body, but cannot break free.

"Aeden," I spit out, recognizing this new foe as Deiniol's cousin on his mother's side. "Why do you help him?"

Aeden laughs. "Drop the weapon, Deiniol. I'll hold the rat while you hit him."

Deiniol's eyes glint alarmingly. They're almost more frightening than the knife he carries. Deiniol takes a step forward, knife outstretched; then tosses it aside into one of the stalls. I smirk. Instantly, I know I've made a mistake and try to tame my expression, but it's too late.

Deiniol's face twists in hatred. He rushes forward and drives his shoulder into me. Aeden has already backed away and Deiniol and I go down: me underneath and Deiniol straddling my abdomen. I rock my hips trying to throw him off. I scrabble my hands on either side for a fistful of hay to throw into his face, but the stable floor is unaccountably clean and smooth. I can feel the restlessness in the horses, as they, in turn, sense my distress. They cannot help me, however, and Deiniol ignores both them and my struggles. He grasps my wrists so tightly my hands go numb and pulls them above my head.

We glare at each other. There's blood on my lip where I bit it and my belly aches from Deiniol's pummels. Still, I don't look away, and at long last Deiniol sees something in me that gives him pause. His eyes narrow and we still.

I can't breathe. Suddenly, Deiniol tips his head back and screams his frustration to the sky. Only then does help come, in the form of Deiniol's mother.

"Boys!" she says, insulting all three of us without thought. "We leave for Mercia tomorrow and yet all you can think to do is scuffle in the dust!"

"So it's true," Aeden says. "Cai has defected to Modred."

"And we with him," my foster mother says.

Deiniol rolls off me. I get to my feet and meet his gaze. "I will remember this, mochyn," he says. It is the word for 'pig', but means bastard. "This is only the beginning."

"Don't be ridiculous," his mother says, brushing straw from Deiniol's shoulders. "Myrddin, I expected better of you."

The unfairness of that leaves me speechless and unable to defend myself. Deiniol smirks at me from behind his mother's back. He tips his head to Aeden and prances after his mother, leaving me alone in the stables.

What Deiniol doesn't realize is that this time, the lesson I've learned is the opposite of the one he intended. When we meet next, four years later, Arthur is in the ascendancy and it is Deiniol, not me, whose stands downcast on the losing side.

"I find that I must travel to Caerhun in the company of my foster father's son. I spoke to you of him yesterday."

Nell's look was sympathetic. "I wish I could come with you instead. I'm useless here."

"That isn't true." Myrddin reached out and smoothed the hair near her forehead. "Besides. It's impossible. You know that."

"This is all new to me," she said. "I'm at loose ends."

"There's an herb garden behind the kitchen," Myrddin said, "and a drying shed beyond. Perhaps you can be of some assistance there."

"Don't—" Nell broke off, swallowing the rest of the sentence. Myrddin watched her carefully as she looked away, took a deep breath, and turned back to him. "I've already found it. You're right. They have need of me here."

Unsure what her cut-short comment would have been but glad that Nell would make an attempt to be content, at least for today, Myrddin inspected the mustering men in the courtyard. The clouds hung low and the rain fell so hard it was like they were standing in a waterfall. He sighed and set out into it. It would be a hideously cold ride to Caerhun.

"You," Deiniol said, as his initial greeting.

They stood beneath the gatehouse archway while a stable boy used a cloth to dry Myrddin's saddle. Deiniol had already mounted and wore his hood pulled tight around his head to counter the rain. Regardless, even wearing wool cloaks, it wouldn't take long for the rain this heavy to soak everyone through.

"Deiniol," Myrddin said.

"I see you haven't changed," he said. "Still a sniveling child with a snotty nose and a craven look about you."

"Sweet Mary." Having pulled up her hood and come to see what kind of man Myrddin despised, Nell spoke sincerely.

"Is that your woman?" Deiniol lifted his chin and pointed it at Nell. "I heard men speak of her in the hall."

Myrddin had an overwhelming urge to drive his fist into Deiniol's face. Nell, perhaps sensing this, moved closer.

"I hear she used to be a nun," Deiniol continued. "You'll have a cold bed to come home to, won't you?"

Now, Nell caught Myrddin's elbow and held on. "I'm a grown woman. I've heard worse, and experienced worse, as you well know. Don't get in trouble on my behalf."

Ifan muttered under his breath, turning towards Myrddin and pretending to inspect the length of his stirrups. "Does he rehearse these insults? A man could take lessons from him."

"It's been many years since I was forced into his company," Myrddin said.

"No doubt this was far too soon for a reunion," Ifan said.

"Twenty miles we've to go today," Myrddin said, "and each one will seem like an eternity."

"He hates you," Nell said.

Myrddin looked into her concerned face, her eyes flicking from Deiniol to him. Fortunately, Deiniol had turned his horse's head and urged him out from under the gatehouse, into the rain. Myrddin had a vision of the tower coming loose and crushing him as he rode beneath it.

"He does," Myrddin said. "I've never known why."

"Some men don't need a reason." Ifan straightened his saddle bags. "Did you say that he's your brother?"

"Foster brother. Don't remind me," Myrddin said.

"No wonder you rabbited about when you first came to the king, jumping at every shadow." Two years older than Myrddin, Ifan had been a squire in Lord Bedwyr's retinue when Myrddin had arrived at Garth Celyn. "I gather it was he who gave you those bruises that were just fading when you came to the king?"

"You never said anything about them. I'd hoped nobody noticed. It wouldn't do for a future knight to reveal so clearly how unable he was to defend himself."

Ifan shrugged, embarrassed perhaps to have brought them up. "You survived, didn't you? Sometimes a man wears bruises because he's the last one standing."

That made Myrddin smile. It was odd to think that he'd spent nearly twenty years in Ifan's company and this was the first Ifan had mentioned the day he'd arrived. It had been a cold day in March, with snow in the mountains. Myrddin had come down the road to Garth Celyn all on his own, with little more than a broken down horse he'd taken from Madoc's stables and his sword, a not-insignificant inheritance from his mother.

The news of Cai's stunning defection had just hit and Garth Celyn had been in upheaval. Arthur had barely glanced at Myrddin, just informed his captain to find him a place to sleep in the barracks, a better horse, and decent armor if he was to be of any use to him at all. King Arthur had needed men and Myrddin had found being treated like a man to his liking.

"By the balls of St. Mari!" Deiniol swore as the rain turned to sleet, and then the first flakes of snow began to coat his shoulders.

Even Ifan blinked twice at that bit of blasphemy and reluctantly mounted his horse. "Would King Arthur be upset if I killed him? We could run him through and throw him into a chasm. No one would be the wiser."

"We'll do it on the way back if we're truly desperate," Myrddin said.

"I'll watch his back, miss." Ifan nodded at Nell, and then turned his horse's head towards the sea to follow Deiniol.

Myrddin lifted Nell's hand from his coat. "I'm five years younger than Deiniol and the last time we spent time in each other's in company was the evening I ran away. He wanted to kill me. It was only the sudden arrival of his mother that stopped him."

"At least Ifan is with you," she said.

Myrddin laughed. "I would have said he would act as a barrier to me killing Deiniol today. But now I'm pretty sure I'll have to get in line."

Nell wrinkled her nose at him. If they hadn't had that conversation the day before about him sleeping across the room from her, Myrddin would have called it coquettish. "You be careful."

"Let's go, *mochyn!*" Deiniol had stopped some forty feet away to wait for Ifan to catch up, and they both twisted in their seats to look for Myrddin. "The Saxons ride away."

Because it was urgent and he was right, Myrddin did as he was asked, telling himself that he was doing the king's will. Myrddin gave a final nod to Nell; then he spurred Cadfarch. The three men rode out of Garth Celyn, heading towards the southern pass.

2

11 November 537 AD

Nell perched on her stool, leaning over the narrow wooden table in front of her. Dried plants hung from the ceiling while herbs and spices crowded the shelves. In short order, she'd made the gardener's shed that lay across the herb garden from the kitchen a haven, installing a warming brazier and cushioned stool, taking Myrddin's advice and making the idea her own. The only light, other than from the brazier, shone from a pewter candelabra in front of her which held three glowing candles. A hole in the roof let out the smoke, but other than that, the room allowed no exterior light. Admittedly, a window would have done her little good, as it was four o'clock in the afternoon and already nearly dark.

"How are you doing?"

Nell looked up as Myrddin entered the hut. She'd been writing on a scrap of vellum, detailing the dream she'd had the previous night. If she closed her eyes, she could see it running in an endless loop behind her eyelids. It came so often now, night after night, that she sometimes felt she was more awake when she was dreaming than the other way around.

"Fine." She straightened, hoping she hadn't given anything away. She wasn't fine, of course. It was hard to see how she was ever going to be fine again. Myrddin, for his part, watched her warily, as if he knew she was lying to him. She hated feeling so vulnerable. She missed those high convent walls, keeping out the world. "How long have you been standing there?"

"Long enough to watch you fill the page. I heard a few phrases that could have been curses, too." Myrddin smiled. "You haven't been spending time among the garrison in my absence, have you? At least Deiniol isn't here to bother you."

She found that she couldn't smile back. It was no laughing matter that Deiniol had ridden with Myrddin and Ifan only as far as the pagan stones before taking a track south into the mountains. They'd let him go alone into the wilderness, rather than lose the Saxon messengers they'd been sent to follow.

Myrddin walked to her and peered over her shoulder, resting one hand on the table beside the inkpot. Nell hunched her shoulders, covering the page with one hand so he couldn't read her words. It was just like him to be able to read too: he pretended to be a bachelor, journeyman knight, but every now and then he would evidence some new, unexpected skill that belied his claim. He couldn't fool her anymore.

He stood at her shoulder, refusing to take the hint. After another count of ten, he sighed and eased away from her. But he didn't leave her alone as she wanted—or part of her wanted and the rest didn't.

"What is it, Nell? Tell me what's bothering you. You can trust me."

She glanced up at him. "It isn't that I don't trust you."

"Isn't it?" he said. "I would like to think that you're telling me the truth this time, but it's hard to tell. I share a room with you, and meals, but you never talk of anything more momentous than the weather. The world is falling in around us; we're in the middle of a war. Why won't you speak of it?"

Nell bowed her head.

Endlessly patient as always, Myrddin leaned against the counter on which she prepared her herbs and ointments.

Finally, she pushed away the paper and turned in her seat to face him. "I'm tired, Myrddin. I'm thirty years old, and I feel a hundred."

"You don't look it." He tried to coax a smile. This time, she obliged, although it quickly faded.

"Why did you come to find me, Myrddin?"

"We've news from Powys," Myrddin said. "Lord Edgar has sent word that he might be persuaded to change sides, given the proper incentives."

Nell stared at him, her stomach sinking into her boots while a vision of the church by the Cam River rose unbidden before her eyes. "That couldn't possibly be true. His family has ever been faithful to the kings of Mercia—and now Modred. Does King Arthur believe it?"

"King Arthur has said nothing to me, but just this morning he sent a captain south to prepare to open a second front against the Saxons—on our terms this time, not Modred's. Geraint told me that given this new approach from Edgar, the king will want to lead his men himself."

Nell shook her head, an iciness taking over her limbs. Ten heartbeats ago she was alone with her dreams and her fears, and now the dream was a reality. "I don't think this is a good idea. Surely the king must see that?"

"The king needs to change the balance of power, and perhaps making Edgar an ally is the way to do it."

"What about—" Nell thought desperately for anything—any idea—that could divert this folly. Twenty years of dreaming and she'd never been this close to the king—or to complete failure. "You have the king's confidence. What if you suggested to the king that he look to someone else to turn aside from Edgar. Someone like Lord Cedric of Brecon. He hates Modred."

In 521, Cedric's father had fought against Modred and Icel, the King of Mercia at the time, in a war over the border territory between Mercia and Wessex. Cedric's family had allied with Arthur, who had some stake in the outcome, though not a large one. But Cedric's father had died of the wounds he received at Shrewsbury and Cedric himself, only sixteen at the time, had witnessed his father's wounding and subsequent death while in Modred's custody.

Myrddin laughed. "He's none too fond of Arthur either," he said. "And he's as mercenary as Cai."

"True," she said. "But he's more open about it. You never have to wonder at his motives. You just need to make sure your goals align with his. And from what I know of the man, he's always been up-front with his allegiances. If he walks away from an alliance with Modred, he'd probably tell him about it in advance, rather than stab him in the back."

"Yes," Myrddin agreed. "But it isn't he who has sent a message to King Arthur."

"But— " Nell stopped. A curious look had passed across Myrddin's face. *Could I have said something right?* "It was his family who sided with King Arthur sixteen years ago. They might do it again."

"Modred forgave Cedric's family their treason." Myrddin nodded as he thought it through. "But the death of a father due to the mercilessness of one's lord is not something any man can easily forget, or forgive, especially one arising from as ancient a lineage as Cedric."

"Arthur wants to unite Wales as its king," Nell said. "Cedric wants his bit of land secure and to stop having to fight either Arthur or his own supposed allies for the right to it. He wants more land too, but it's unlikely that Modred is going to award him any more—not any time soon."

"The land would be at the expense of Agravaine, Aelric, or Edgar," Myrddin said, "staunch allies of Modred."

"Well, except possibly for Edgar," Nell said.

"And you say that, why?"

"Because Edgar is—" Nell paused and pursed her lips, uncertain as to whether or not she should say more.

"Edgar is what?"

"Edgar does not prefer women," Nell said, as delicately as she could. "To my mind, this is why Modred has withheld Edgar's inheritance since his father died. None of the Mercian barons think Edgar is a fit heir, but it *is* his right."

"And how do you know all this?"

Nell stared at the floor, biting her bottom lip. She had so many things to tell him; so many things he might not forgive or understand.

Myrddin waited through the silence.

Finally, Nell waved a hand, apologetically, unable to avoid revealing to him this bit of the truth. "My husband served as a man-at-arms at Wigmore Castle."

Myrddin gaped at her. "He was part of the garrison? For Edgar's family?"

Nell couldn't mistake the anger and distrust that rose in his face—the same distrust he'd felt that first night on the road from St. Asaph. "Yes."

"Why didn't you tell me this before?"

"Because you're a staunch supporter of Arthur!" Nell's voice went high and tears pricked at her eyes in her anxiety. "You thought I was a spy! How could I tell you my husband served a Saxon lord?" A lone tear fell across her cheek and she angrily brushed it away with the back of her hand.

"I already suspected the worst," Myrddin said. "It would have confirmed my suspicions."

"And you still have them now." Her heart sank.

"No man can ever truly know what is in another's soul." Myrddin was unrelenting. "Was your husband Saxon?"

"No." Nell crossed her arms and stared at the floor. "Many of the men-at-arms who serve the Saxons are Welsh."

"So who was he?"

Nell closed her eyes. "His name was Rhys. He was ten years older than I, the younger son of a landowner who held lands to the south of my father's." She'd been such a child when she married him. Not so much foolish, but innocent, in love with the handsome soldier she barely knew, even if she'd known him from infancy, but sure of her future with him. "Fifteen years ago there was peace between Wales and Mercia and my father didn't object to the marriage."

"But you didn't want to stay?" Myrddin said. "Once your husband and children died?"

"No," Nell said. "I didn't. I told you that before and it was nothing but the truth. It was Edgar, in fact, who helped me return to Wales."

"And you haven't been back since?" Myrddin said.

"No."

"And Edgar?" Myrddin said. "Have you a further thought, then, about his message to King Arthur?"

"I don't know about that," Nell said. "It's Agravaine who has the real power. Modred put him in charge of all his forces, including Edgar's, for a reason. I wouldn't be surprised if the letter to the king was Agravaine's idea, and Edgar was only going along with the deception because he wanted to prove to Modred his loyalty—to force him to acknowledge that he is his father's rightful heir."

"That is my thought too," Myrddin said. "If Arthur goes to meet Edgar, I fear he goes to his death."

Nell had been studying her toes, not looking at Myrddin as he interrogated her. Now she glanced up, surprised that he would say such a thing so openly and surely. "I feel that too. Can you think of a way to stop him? I will help you if I can!"

Myrddin studied her face and she let him, not looking away. His lips twisted. "We'll see." With a last nod, he spun on one heel and left the hut.

Nell stared after him. When his footsteps had faded, she leaned her head back against wall and closed her eyes. In twenty years of dreaming, nothing she'd tried had turned out right. This was obviously not working either. Perhaps she shouldn't have allowed Myrddin to bring her to Garth Celyn after all.

3

As he stared up at the battlements of Rhuddlan Castle, Myrddin felt for the letter from King Arthur to Modred one last time, as reassurance. Arthur had selected him to bring it as he'd promised. Myrddin had come alone because in the end, the king had determined that it was better to lose one man to an early grave or Modred's dungeon than a company of them.

"I'm not too happy about this either, Nell," Myrddin had said, standing in Garth Celyn's courtyard that morning. Nell had held Cadfarch's bridle and fed him carrots while Myrddin adjusted his saddlebags. "Nor is the king."

"Take me with you," she said. "Nobody will know or care if I leave here, or what happens to me."

"I will care." Myrddin wouldn't soon forget her tears from yesterday and their effect on his heart. "The road I'm taking passes right through St. Asaph. You don't need to ride through there again."

"Maybe I do need to," Nell said.

"Nell—"

"I wouldn't be alone this time," Nell said. "I'd be with you, and I'd pretend to be your little brother. Nobody would give me a second look."

"In boy's clothes?" Myrddin said.

"Of course."

"No," he said, more firmly than before. "You're a nun."

"Not anymore," she said, "and I have no intention of ever being one again."

"The law—"

"*The woman shall not wear that which pertaineth unto a man, neither shall a man put on a woman's garment: for all that do so are abomination unto the Lord thy God,*" Nell quoted. "Give me credit for knowing at least that. But with Eryri about to fall to Modred, wearing a boy's discarded breeches is surely a small matter."

She gazed at him, disconcerting him because a vision of her lifeless and abused body had risen before his eyes. He blinked to clear them before she realized he'd seen it. That she'd experienced attempted rape and murder even once was unconscionable. She was crazed to think Myrddin would let her near the scene of the crime again.

"It wouldn't work." Regardless of his opinion, the request was ludicrous and she had to know it. But Myrddin understood it, too. She was a vibrant and competent woman, adrift in the middle of a war; little wonder that she was struggling with it. But riding with him wasn't the answer.

"It isn't because you don't trust me, is it?" she said. "It's not because you still believe that I spy for Modred?"

"That's not it," Myrddin said, acknowledging at last, albeit grudgingly, that the idea had always been unlikely.

"Besides." Nell changed tack. "Masterless men didn't attack me. Those men were knights. I just happened to get in their way."

Myrddin snorted under his breath. "Don't you think I know that? Modred would never allow marauders so close to Rhuddlan. His men are disciplined and he would have taken care of any such men who'd dared roam his territory. But who's going to *be* at Rhuddlan? Those very same men! The thought of you left to your own devices at Rhuddlan Castle sends chills down my spine."

Nell studied his face and then sighed, backing down. "Yes, my lord."

Myrddin's eyes narrowed at her uncharacteristic use of his title.

Her shoulders fell for a second, but then she poked him in the chest. "But I'm holding it against you."

"I can accept that," Myrddin had said. He'd glanced back once as he left the castle to see Nell and Ifan standing on the battlements, watching him ride away. Nell had tucked herself into her cloak, with the hood up, but Ifan stood bareheaded, his crop of short, blonde hair unmistakable. Each had lifted a hand to wave him down the road. Myrddin had responded with a salute.

Now, at sunset, he followed the western side of the Clwyd River, past the drawbridge and its lesser gate, to the ford. Cadfarch splashed through the river, came up the bank, and stopped in front of the main defensive tower in the outer palisade. Myrddin waited, hoping that the archers who peered at him from the battlements would remain patient. He was Welsh but that didn't mean that he was an enemy. Sad, but true.

A guard called to him from the walkway above the gatehouse. "Give me your name and your purpose." The man, tall and helmetless, spoke in heavily accented Welsh.

"I come at the request of Arthur ap Uther, King of Wales," Myrddin said, answering him in Saxon, the language in which he was sure to be most comfortable. "I have a letter for Lord Modred."

The man studied Myrddin and then nodded. "You may enter," he said, now in flawless Saxon, confirming Myrddin's assessment, "provided you surrender your weapons."

Myrddin agreed with reluctance to what the soldier asked. Men wore weapons as a matter of course and for a man *not* to wear his sword was unusual—and insulting to the unarmed man, which is of course why the soldier intended to strip Myrddin of his. It wasn't that he feared Myrddin would use his sword against Modred, but because he sought to humiliate him, and by association, King Arthur.

Myrddin urged Cadfarch under the gatehouse and into the outer bailey. Once inside the curtain wall, a cobbled path led to the massive double towers of the second gatehouse which protected the great hall behind it. Modred's fort was impregnable. No one had ever taken it by force, although not for lack of trying. Cai had attacked it after taking down one of Modred's more eastern castles the previous spring, but other than causing some damage from fire, he'd gone away unsatisfied. It might be possible to starve the defenders out, but Myrddin wouldn't have been surprised to learn that Modred had built an escape tunnel under his castle, just like at Garth Celyn. Then again, he had less experience in losing wars and so perhaps hadn't thought he needed one.

Torches flared in sconces—dozens of them—lighting the bailey almost as if it were day. Like everything else about Rhuddlan, the expansive light was a display of wealth and power that the local populace would surely notice. Compared to any of King Arthur's castles, which tended to be coldly utilitarian, even if their castellans did everything they could to make them comfortable, Rhuddlan was a palace. Modred's image of himself had only grown more resplendent as his victories had increased in number.

Myrddin dismounted and instantly three men were upon him, two gripping his upper arms while a third disarmed him. He patted Myrddin down, finding one knife in his boot and a second tucked into the bracer on his forearm. Myrddin had hoped they'd miss that one and kicked himself for not having a maid sew a smaller knife into the lining of his cloak. A true spy, he wasn't. Perhaps it was time he learned.

Just as they finished, another man—of obvious rank, given his clothing and the artistry in the hilt of his sword— came out from under the secondary gatehouse. Even his walk was purposeful and distinctive. The men sitting outside the stables with doxies on their laps hastily put them aside to stand at his approach. The man didn't indicate that he noticed, although Myrddin guessed that if he was a captain worth his salt, he would confront them later. When the man reached Myrddin, he gave Myrddin a curt nod and said, "Lord Mordred will see you now."

Myrddin hadn't expected anything different in terms of courtesy, although it would have been nice to brush the dust from his clothes and polish himself up so as to represent Arthur better. With no help for it, he allowed a stable boy to lead Cadfarch away and then trailed after the man, followed by one of the men-at-arms carrying his weapons. Even Modred knew he couldn't have his men toss them in a corner—that Myrddin wouldn't countenance it. They were his livelihood and the value of the sword alone was that of an entire village.

Rhuddlan's walls and towers loomed even larger from the ground than on horseback. As Myrddin followed the knight through the second gatehouse, the second bailey, and into the great hall, he had to shake his head over the amount of time and treasure it had taken to build it. Modred's people must be suffering greatly to have given him so much in such a short time.

The hall was full of men at their evening meal. Myrddin and his escort by-passed them, however, and headed down a corridor to Modred's receiving room. The metal fittings of Myrddin's boots clacked loudly on the stones as he paced along the corridor, a match to the pounding of his heart which seemed to rise farther into his throat with every step. Then he told himself that if he was to turn aside the fate set for Wales in the dream, if he was to become the man Arthur needed him to be, he'd have to do better.

When facing down an enemy, whether Deiniol as a boy or a hated upstart nobleman, confidence was everything. Much as Nell had done when she'd first spoken to King Arthur back at Garth Celyn, Myrddin replaced uncertainty with pride. Straightening his shoulders, Myrddin nodded at the man who'd brought him. The man's eyes crinkled at the corners, acknowledging the transition Myrddin had affected, and nodded back.

The man threw open the door to Modred's receiving room. It was the same size as the great hall at Garth Celyn, but as it was only a third as large as the hall Myrddin had just come through, Modred used it for his private meetings. Not that this was going to be private. Myrddin had walked into a room full of people and had their immediate attention. Deliberately ignoring everyone but the man in charge, Myrddin strode towards Modred. He no longer had a sword at his waist but he held a missive of defiance close to his heart, which was almost the same thing, and perhaps better.

His heart caught in his throat, however, at the sight of Archbishop Dafydd standing to Modred's right. Myrddin hadn't realized, even with all the discussion of peace lately, that the two men were so close—and that Modred had this level of support from the Church. For his part, the Archbishop observed Myrddin as he came to a halt five paces from Modred's throne, with its gilt frame, raised dais, and thick rug. Myrddin bowed, straightened, his hands at his sides, and looked straight at Modred.

"Come," Modred said. "Let's see what my beloved uncle has to say to me today."

Modred appeared exactly as he should, which was to say, like a king. He was forty years old, into middle-age, but didn't look it. He had a full head of dark hair, broad shoulders, and eyes that Myrddin would have avoided if he could. It was hard not to think they saw right through him. *Christ, I hate him.* Still upright, refusing to allow his thoughts to show, Myrddin advanced towards Modred's throne. He removed the letter from his breast pocket and with a second, short bow, held it out to Modred.

"My lord," Myrddin said. "King Arthur greets you and hopes that his royal nephew is well."

"How kind of him to inquire." Modred took the letter, watching Myrddin out of the corner of his eye as he did so, and broke the seal. He unrolled it and read for no more than a count of ten. Without re-rolling it, Modred handed the letter to the Archbishop, who took it. Myrddin kept his hands relaxed at his sides, wondering what would happen next. He didn't like the feeling he was getting from Modred or his lackeys, many of whom were watching him like he was a rare beast in a cage. Or a chicken intended for slaughter.

While the Archbishop read Arthur's letter, Modred sat still, his only movement the tapping of his finger on the arm of his chair as he waited. He didn't appear disturbed or angry by King Arthur's words, just impatient. The letter seemed no more or less than what he had expected.

"And Cai's response?" Modred said.

Myrddin had that letter too. He didn't know precisely what it said, but suspected it was far less polite than Arthur's. "Here, my lord." Myrddin pulled it from his pocket and handed it to Modred.

Modred took it, split the seal, and passed it off so quickly to the Archbishop he couldn't have read more than three words. Instead, he revealed that he had other things on his mind. "And what was your role in the battle at the Strait?"

Myrddin blinked, nonplussed. And then decided the question wasn't so surprising. Very few of Modred's men had survived the battle, and perhaps he hadn't yet had a good first-hand account. "I am one of the knights in my king's household guard," Myrddin said, deciding there was no harm in telling him this bit of truth. Eventually he'd hear it from someone else. "I was at the forefront of the initial charge."

"Tell me what happened," Modred said.

Myrddin took in a breath. Modred would hate what he had to say, but then, it was unlikely Myrddin's explanation could make it worse for him. "The Saxon forces crossed the Strait at noon on November 6th. Once the cavalry reached the beach and the foot soldiers were marching on the bridge, we unleashed our arrows." Myrddin stopped.

"And then?" Modred watched Myrddin's face. The silence in the hall was complete.

"And then we charged," Myrddin said.

"Who killed Wulfere?" Modred said.

Myrddin hesitated. "I did."

A pause. Unaccountably, Modred smiled. Then he began to laugh. He continued, tears spilling out of his eyes and rolling down his cheeks. After a moment of stunned silence, the rest of the people in the room began to laugh too, even if they, as Myrddin, had no idea what their lord thought was so funny.

Myrddin remained standing in front of Modred. He shared a quick look with the Archbishop, who was the only other person not in hysterics. Then he glanced at the stars beginning to show through the glass in the window to his left. As in the courtyard, the wealth on display in the hall was palpable, from the glass in the windows, to the dual fireplaces, one on each side of the hall, to the tapestries that adorned the walls. Myrddin wished he was gone already but until the king dismissed him, he had to stay. Finally, Modred calmed enough to explain himself.

"Your king has quite a sense of humor," he said. "He sends his letter with the one man he knows I won't touch. He probably thinks I should thank you for doing to Wulfere what I would have done myself, except that you robbed me of my pleasure."

"My lord, my apologies if I displeased you, but Wulfere attacked me." Myrddin bowed again, for lack of anything better to do or say. Wulfere had disobeyed a direct order. If he hadn't lost his life at the Strait, if Modred was angry enough, he might have hung him from the tallest tower at Rhuddlan and afterwards stuck his head on a pike for display. On the whole, given Modred's cruel streak, Myrddin had done Wulfere a favor.

Modred barked another laugh. "No regrets, eh?" He fingered his lip. "To repay the loss of my prize, you can render me a small service while you're here, especially as you appear so adept at delivering messages."

"If I can, my lord," Myrddin said.

"Lord Cedric of Brecon awaits my pleasure," he said. "I think I've kept him waiting long enough. Bring him to me."

"Certainly, sir," Myrddin said.

He turned on his heel, his mind racing. *What a gift! The very man he'd wanted to meet*! Nell would have his head if he didn't take advantage of the opportunity—he almost wished he'd brought her with him to help him think of what to say. Myrddin marched towards the door, the space between his shoulder blades tingling with the force of the glare that he felt Modred directing at him. He would have run from the room if he could, but as it was, the instant Myrddin cleared the doorway, he heaved a sigh of relief.

Myrddin had no idea where Modred was keeping Cedric, whether in the dungeon, or the tower, or a private suite. It was a simple matter, however, to ask a servant, who gave him directions and informed him, as a by-the-way, that Cedric had arrived by boat just after dawn and had been cooling his heels in his rooms ever since, waiting for Modred to send for him.

To give Modred credit, he *was* treating Cedric as an honored guest. Given the disaster at the Strait, coupled with the fact that the two men hated each other, that was somewhat surprising. Still, Cedric had remained overtly loyal to Modred and was a high ranking nobleman—and Modred's cousin—even if every task he performed for Modred was accomplished with great loathing.

As Myrddin approached Cedric's rooms, a disturbing amount of mumbling and shouting began leaking through the half-open door into the passage. He fought his instinct to run into the room to quiet the man. Didn't Cedric realize he was in enemy territory? Didn't he see the need to bury his emotions and keep his thoughts more private?

"Fools!" Cedric's voice echoed down the corridor. "The indignity of being forced to wait in my rooms! To have my honor called into question!"

Myrddin arrived in Cedric's doorway, knocked, and then took a step back so as not to crowd the threshold. Booted feet echoed on the floor and Cedric himself opened the door. Beyond, the room was empty.

"Lord Cedric." Myrddin bowed and pretended he hadn't overheard him. "Lord Modred requests your presence."

At the sight of Myrddin, Cedric's face transformed from rage to a blank and expressionless façade—all except for his eyes, which glinted, the sole indication of the fire behind them. He glared at Myrddin and then slid the sword he'd been brandishing at his unseen listeners into the sheath at his waist.

"Finally," he said. "Is the Archbishop beside him?"

"Yes, my lord," Myrddin said.

"And who are you?" He pointed his chin at Myrddin. "By your features, you are a Welshmen, yet your Saxon is perfect."

"Myrddin. A knight in the retinue of King Arthur ap Uther."

That got Cedric's attention. He examined Myrddin through narrowed eyes. Then he tipped his face to study the rafters above him and spoke in a low voice. "Why does Modred send you to me? What is it that I don't know?"

"I came to Rhuddlan because I bore a message from my king to Modred." Myrddin answered him even if the question had been rhetorical—and then decided that he would take advantage of the opportunity Modred had given him. Maybe there really was a way to prevent Arthur from meeting Lord Edgar at that damned church a month from now. "But it is well that Lord Modred sent me here, for I have a query for you on behalf of my king."

Cedric's head came down at that and he looked at Myrddin warily. He pushed past Myrddin to look both ways down the hall, and then gave Myrddin a curt nod. "Tell me quickly."

"You and King Arthur have been at odds," Myrddin said. "He would rather you were allies."

Cedric pursed his lips and looked away. He contemplated the hilt of his sword on which he rested his left hand and tapped a staccato with one finger at its end, in a similar thinking pose to Modred's. Then, moving quickly into the hall, Cedric caught a courtier off-guard who was hurrying down it. The man bowed low as he reached Cedric, and then continued on.

Unable to read Cedric and wondering how big a mistake he'd made, Myrddin turned to follow him. Myrddin assumed that Cedric expected him to walk behind him, given Myrddin's nationality and as befitting Cedric's rank which was so much higher than Myrddin's. Once the courtier had disappeared around a far corner, however, Cedric motioned impatiently for Myrddin to come abreast. Myrddin did as he asked and the two men walked together down the passage. Or rather, Myrddin walked, and Cedric stalked.

"What is his mood?" Cedric didn't need to explain whose mood he meant. Apparently they were going to ignore King Arthur's supposed message.

"I have no idea," Myrddin said. "The Archbishop stood beside him and said nothing either. I can't imagine Modred was happy with Archbishop Dafydd's attempts to mediate a peace settlement, but he would never reveal what he is thinking—to anyone perhaps, but certainly not to one of King Arthur's men."

Cedric grunted, but whether that meant agreement or disapproval, Myrddin didn't know. Then, as they approached Modred's receiving room, Cedric slowed. "You have served King Arthur for many years?"

"Yes."

"Does he strike you as a man with a temper?"

Myrddin glanced warily at him, not sure where this was leading. "No. He has one, of course, but when it rises he turns cold, not hot."

Cedric nodded. "Lord Modred is not one to cross. For me to do so would have ramifications for generations to come. You tell that to your lord."

Uncertain, Myrddin stood frozen to the floor for the half a second it took Cedric to push open the door leading to Modred's rooms. Then, galvanized by Cedric's retreating back, Myrddin hurried after him as Cedric crossed the twenty feet to where Modred sat, no longer on his throne but behind a desk that was set under one of the windows to the left of the central fireplace.

Modred had emptied the hall in Myrddin's absence. Now, Archbishop Dafydd was the only other man present. Both Archbishop and Lord Modred had been bent over a piece of paper, which the Archbishop now folded and slid into a hidden pocket beneath his robes. It was warmer in the room than before, despite the fewer bodies to heat it. The fires had been stoked and blazed brightly. Like Arthur, Modred had the best of everything. The remains of dinner lay on the corner of his table. The Archbishop held a goblet of wine and a hint of spice wafted from it.

Cedric reached Modred and bowed at the precisely correct angle that was required. In contrast, Myrddin's feet stuck to the floor just inside the doorway, near the bench where his untended weapons lay. For a heartbeat, Myrddin considered grabbing his sword and making a run for it. One glance at the guards by the open door who had shifted to more ready stances had him biding his time a while longer. The exit was a long way away, through the great hall and two well-guarded gatehouses. If Myrddin was going to reach it, it wasn't going to be at a flat-out run. Stealth would have to be the order the of day.

"You summoned me, sire?" Cedric said.

Modred leaned back in his chair and for a count of ten sat unmoving, elbows resting on the arms, seemingly relaxed. Cedric's words hung in the air as Modred left his question unanswered. Cedric waited with what appeared to be patience for his lord's response.

"Tell me of the defeat at the Menai Strait," Modred said, finally, as if discussing the dreadful weather, and as if he hadn't just asked Myrddin the same question half an hour before.

"My lord—" Cedric began.

Modred cut him off, leaning forward to punctuate his next words with a pointing finger. "Explain to me why so many of my men are dead: Wulfere, Golm, Halfric, Dane, not to mention the equipment and horses that are now at the bottom of the sea! Do you understand the huge expenses I am incurring in this business? Of the criminal waste that this defeat has entailed?" By the end of his query, Modred's voice had risen to the point where the sound buffeted Cedric like waves.

"Wulfere refused to listen to me." Cedric lifted his chin, aiming to withstand the onslaught. "He, not I, was the commander in the field. He, not I, is to blame for the loss of so many of our men."

"And he, not you, paid for his error with his life." Modred sat back in his chair as if he'd never raised his voice. "By the sword of our friend, here." He gestured with one hand towards Myrddin. Cedric's eyes met Myrddin's. The corner of Cedric's mouth twitched before his face blanked and he turned back to his lord.

"As you say, my lord." Cedric bowed his head and then raised it to meet Modred's eyes. "I tried to convince Wulfere and the others that you would not countenance an attack on that day, not with the Archbishop in the middle of negotiations and hoping for a settlement between you and King Arthur. Wulfere thought he could ensure that a settlement was unnecessary. He supposed that a great victory could convince Arthur to submit to you, or at best, he could capture the king by driving down the coast to Garth Celyn, once he'd navigated the bridge. Regardless, he refused to listen to my cautions."

From what Myrddin knew of both Cedric and Wulfere, he believed Cedric's story. Myrddin had to wonder, however, how hard Cedric had tried to get Wulfere to change course. He must have despised Wulfere—everyone did. Even Modred couldn't have admired the man as a person. He had put

Wulfere in charge of his troops because he could be trusted to get the job done.

That alone had to have been a huge sore point for Cedric, whom Modred had overlooked from the start of the war in favor of Agravaine in particular. To have put Wulfere in charge of the men on Anglesey added insult to injury. To Cedric's mind, if Wulfere had won the battle, Cedric could have gone along with it; if Wulfere made a fool of himself, Cedric wouldn't have been at fault. Nobody could have foreseen the total disaster the battle had become for the Saxons.

"On the day of the attack, a fault in the bridge of boats delayed us," Cedric said, continuing his story. "Wulfere had intended to cross at dawn but ended up crossing at noon. It was the optimal time, with the water high, but as we traversed the bridge, we failed to surprise the Welsh forces. They caught us on the beach, low ground, between the trees and the water. When we retreated, the swift waters of the Strait and the weight of the horses and equipment on the bridge ensured our near total defeat."

"And gave Arthur new reason to resist me." Modred surged to his feet. Myrddin would have said he was furious, but as always, his eyes remained cold, revealing nothing of the man inside. "He sits in his eyrie in Snowdonia, mocking me, as if I haven't the power to root him out! I will accept nothing less from that bastard king than complete submission!"

If the back of Myrddin's knees had not been resting on the edge of the bench, he would have taken a step back at the king's vehemence. Even Cedric, for all his confidence, thought better of any reply. Myrddin decided not to mention that Arthur, of all the Welsh lords, appeared to have been born legitimate.

For Modred's part, he wasn't done. "Arthur is arrogant! Impossible! Look at the letter he sends me!" Modred leaned over the desk and shoved one of the pieces of parchment towards Cedric who just managed to catch it before it fell from the table. Unrolling the paper, he studied the words in silence, but Myrddin knew well what they said:

... we are ready to come to the Archbishop's grace, if it is offered in a form safe and honourable for us. But the form contained in the articles which were sent to us, is in no particular either safe or honourable ... indeed, so far from it that all who hear it are astonished, since it tends rather to the destruction and ruin of our people and our person than to our honour and safety ... for never would our nobles and

subjects consent in the inevitable destruction and dissipation that would surely derive from it ...

Cedric handed the letter back to Modred who tossed it into a wooden box on the floor behind him and sat heavily in his chair once again.

"My spies inform me that Arthur has sent men south to open a new front against me in Powys," Modred said.

Myrddin started at that, the pit forming in his stomach and the chills running down his spine telling him that Modred's attitude towards him had changed in the time he'd been gone. Myrddin gritted his teeth, fighting back the cold certainty. Despite what Modred had said earlier about not harming him because he'd killed Wulfere, he must have decided Myrddin would never leave Rhuddlan or he would not have spoken openly of this. Myrddin was a walking dead man.

"I've heard that Lord Gawain is marshalling a force to threaten Brecon," Cedric said.

"You wish to be relieved of your duties in the north, then?" Modred said. "To deal with this new threat?"

Myrddin couldn't tell if he was mocking Cedric or asking a serious question. Cedric treated it as genuine.

"If it please you, my lord. A strong hand is needed at Brecon or my lands might fall to Arthur's army. That would serve neither me nor you."

Modred contemplated Cedric's face. Cedric, for his part, kept his back straight, looking forward, even if it might cost him Modred's favor. Modred tapped one finger to his lips, as was his habit, and spoke.

"I will not have a repeat of the Anglesey disaster. I had ordered Wulfere to delay his attack. It is fortunate for him that our friend, here, killed him before I could myself."

"I understand completely, my lord," Cedric said. "If I offended you in any way, it was not my intent."

"Is that so?" If anything, Modred grew more still. No doubt, he was thinking, as Myrddin was, of that long ago war. "It is I, and I alone, who will determine that."

"Yes, my lord." Cedric's jaw was set and he spoke through gritted teeth. "I have further news, sire, that might interest you. Lord Edgar has sent a letter to Arthur, inviting him south. If the king wasn't already resolved to lead his men himself, this will confirm his intent."

Was there anything the Saxons didn't know?

Modred leaned forward, apparently truly interested for the first time. "The king has agreed to this meeting?"

"I know not, my lord."

Modred sat back. "Arthur will agree. I am sure of it." Modred sneered. "He is that desperate—and naïve. The notion that Edgar would side with a rebel such as he is laughable."

Cedric didn't respond to Modred's assertion any more than Myrddin did, even if Cedric's mind had to be revolving with the same calculations as Myrddin's. Did Modred know that Edgar's resentments were as great as Cedric's own, for all he was younger and less experienced? Did Modred know of Edgar's anger at being denied his inheritance?

"May I go, my lord?" Cedric bowed yet again.

"Go." Modred waved his hand dismissively. "When we meet next, Arthur will be dead and I will have all Wales in the palm of my hand."

Cedric bowed one more time and turned for the door. He held Myrddin's gaze as he walked the thirty feet between them. Myrddin couldn't read his expression, but felt he was trying to tell him something. His eyes flicked to the door and then back to Myrddin.

Flee now?

If Arthur died, Wales would be left rudderless. Arthur had no sons to come after him and his death would solidify Edgar's station with Modred. The thought could not have been comforting to Cedric. He had to despise Modred's vision of the future of Wales. For Myrddin's part, he didn't like Modred's confident power. He didn't like it at all.

4

13 November 537 AD

The hours after midnight can be bleak. Certainly, the dungeon under the southwest tower of Rhuddlan Castle was not an enjoyable location in which to spend them. The castle was new, true, but the walls seeped water, which came from either the moat or the river—it hardly mattered which one, but given Myrddin's location, he suspected the river—and mold had formed in the corners of his cell. From his fixed position on the wall, he could smell it, although not see it, since darkness shrouded his cell. The sole light came from the torch in a sconce on the wall in the guardroom on the other side of the door.

The door had a hole cut in it, bifurcated by a single bar. Beyond it, the shadows and the occasional figures of Myrddin's guard passed. Representing almost a greater threat than the guards were the three rats that had found their way to a far corner. Those, Myrddin could see as well as hear and they ensured that any notion of dropping off to sleep in such an uncomfortable position was squashed before he took it seriously.

He was still cursing himself as to how in the hell he'd ended up here in the first place.

After Modred had dismissed Cedric, Myrddin had snatched up his weapons and followed Cedric out the door. With a confidence he didn't really feel, Myrddin had moved along the hallway, buckling on his sword and intending to make a quick getaway. Cedric heard his steps behind him, however, and pulled Myrddin aside.

"Modred won't let you leave."

"I fear you are correct," Myrddin said, "but I must try."

"Wait a while," he said. "Dine with me. After the meal, I'll see what I can do for you."

Myrddin doubted he could trust him, but believed the guards would prevent him from walking out the front gate. So Myrddin went to the great hall with Cedric. Full darkness had descended shortly after he'd arrived at Rhuddlan, and by now they'd missed the bulk of the meal. But like Modred, Cedric got to eat whenever he wanted.

The hall was still full of men, all of whom would have been hostile to Myrddin if they'd known who he was. But since he entered as Cedric's new-found companion, if not friend, nobody approached them. Cedric was known for standing on ceremony and insisting on the comforts and accolades of his office—much like King Arthur.

A servant appeared with trenchers for their food and goblets for wine, which she laid before them. She wore the garb of a Saxon girl and was perhaps one of the villagers whom Modred had imported to Rhuddlan for this purpose. Although she was young and lovely, in a blonde, Saxon way, Cedric didn't spare her a glance. It supported the rumors Myrddin had heard that he was faithful to his wife—an unusual trait among noble men. And something else he didn't share with Modred, although Modred apparently did love his wife to distraction.

Myrddin shifted in his seat, peering around the room. "Is Agravaine here?" He'd never met the man and wanted to see what he looked like.

"No," Cedric said, without looking around. He ate with small, dainty bites, as if he wasn't quite sure as to the safety or spicing of the food. "He'd sleep in a barn rather than stay at Rhuddlan."

"Why is that?" Myrddin said.

"The man's a ghost; flitting in and out among Modred's possessions, never stopping anywhere for more than a day if the castle belongs to someone other than himself. Agravaine trusts no one. Modred puts up with it because he wins battles and does as he's told. Half the time it seems he can see the future before it happens."

Myrddin didn't like the sound of that and would have inquired further, but Cedric was done with the subject, taking a sip of wine and then gesturing to the servant for more turnips. Myrddin went back to surveying the hall. Plenty of Welshmen were scattered among the diners—both men who'd sided with Modred from the first and recent defectors. Beyond Cedric's left shoulder, two monks whom Myrddin thought he recognized sat at a far table.

A quick inspection of their undyed robes and cloaks confirmed his suspicions: they were the brothers Llywelyn and Rhys, cousins to Gareth, and brothers to the Hywel who'd died at Penrhyn after the battle at the Strait. Brother Llywelyn was the prior of the monastery at Bangor, and Rhys was the friar of St. Deiniol, the cathedral church, also in Bangor.

As Hywel had explained, it was Llywelyn who'd talked his brothers into betraying King Arthur. Myrddin's disgust for him and that loathsome act hadn't abated in the intervening years. Perhaps feeling the intensity of Myrddin's stare, Llywelyn glanced up, caught Myrddin's eye, and glowered. Once Rhys noted Llywelyn's attention, he turned to look at him as well. Myrddin didn't glance away, but returned their glares. It was childish of him but he refused to back down.

"What are you looking at?" Cedric said, noting Myrddin's odd behavior. He twisted in his seat to glance behind him.

"I know those two monks over there." Myrddin pointed at them with his chin.

Cedric pursed his lips, turning back to his food. "I don't like traitors. Not even ones on my side."

"I suppose it's a matter of perspective," Myrddin said. "One man's traitor is another man's loyal subject."

"Edgar won't betray Lord Modred." Cedric spoke as if they'd had a conversation about Edgar already which had been interrupted, even though they hadn't. "If Modred keeps Agravaine on a tight leash, Agravaine keeps an even tighter one on Edgar. He will do nothing of his own accord."

"Would that be true for you as well?" Myrddin said.

Cedric pointed his knife at Myrddin. "Don't let King Arthur come south."

Myrddin canted his head to the side. "And leave your lands alone?"

Cedric chuckled deep in his throat, but then cut it off. "I'd prefer it."

"What would Modred think of your warning?"

Cedric gave Myrddin a hard look. "He's the one who allowed you to hear of the danger that awaits your king in Powys. Weren't you paying attention earlier? I've not said anything that he hasn't already made clear."

Myrddin shook his head at the complexity of it all. His visions were incomplete and by now, nearly useless. He'd accepted that he had to take action, but while the dreams told him that Arthur shouldn't come south to meet with Edgar, they didn't tell him what would need to happen instead. To have Cedric informing him of what he already knew—even though it hadn't yet happened—was disconcerting.

Cedric pushed away his plate, the food on it half-eaten. He was gathering himself to get to his feet when Modred strode into the room, trailed by the Archbishop. He, in turn, was flanked by two more churchmen whom Myrddin didn't recognize, and said as much to Cedric.

"Bishop Anian of St. Asaph." Cedric rose to his feet as they always did in the presence of Modred. "The other is the Archdeacon of Anglesey."

Myrddin's heart sank into his boots, for he knew what was coming, just as King Arthur had predicted to his brother.

At Modred's raised hand, the room quieted. Modred lifted his voice so that it carried to the far corners of the hall.

"I present to you Archbishop Dafydd. Listen well and take heed of his words."

The Archbishop stepped forward, a piece of paper in his shaking hands. Maybe it was because he suffered from palsy, even though he couldn't have been much older than Myrddin, but Myrddin was willing to believe he understood the significance of what he was about to do and half-regretted it. Myrddin briefly felt sorry for him. Dafydd spoke in Latin, and then again in Saxon so everyone in the room would understand:

Arthur ap Uther, along with his brother, Cai, notwithstanding the formal canonical warning of 17 June last and the repeated appeals to desist from their intentions, have performed a schismatical act of disobedience and have therefore incurred the penalty of excommunication latae sententiae. The priests and faithful are warned not to support the schism of Arthur and Cai, otherwise they shall incur ipso facto a similar punishment.

There it was. Arthur was a devout believer, and would care—fearing for his soul—but this pronouncement would change nothing. The churches in Gwynedd—as opposed to those Archbishop Dafydd oversaw in the south of Wales—would continue to administer to the faithful: marrying, baptizing, and seeing to their spiritual needs, in defiance of the injustice of this act.

"This will make it easier for those who are so inclined to betray King Arthur." Cedric sat down again as Modred left the hall and the priests found seats at the high table.

Myrddin shrugged. "Or the opposite. The excommunication of their leader at the behest of a despised usurper might only confirm the rightness of their choice in their eyes."

"Did you say 'despised usurper'?" Cedric said. "You are too bold."

"A man must live by his conscience," Myrddin said. "When men say that they speak for God, in pursuit of their own power, it calls their words into doubt."

Cedric's hard look was back. Myrddin thought better of further conversation, but even if he'd wanted to speak, he wasn't given a chance. Two men-at-arms appeared, one on either side of Myrddin, grasped him under the arms, and lifted him bodily over his bench. Before Myrddin had a chance to do more than sputter, they had him up against the wall, his back braced and his legs spread.

"What's this?" Cedric gestured with his knife. "We were eating."

The man on Myrddin's right spoke. "Our apologies, my lord. Lord Modred has given orders."

In those first moments of his captivity, his face already bruised from the guard's fists, Myrddin had hoped he could withstand their treatment and not submit. It was clear fairly quickly, however, that they didn't want any information from him. Perhaps they beat prisoners—and King Arthur's men—as a matter of course.

Five hours later, Myrddin's body was stiff from the cold, his wrists and ankles chained, and he had an almighty headache. The one positive note was that the blood along Myrddin's upper lip had dried and was no longer dripping onto his clothing and the floor. He didn't want to attract those rats to his toes, which absent his boots, were too easily accessible. Myrddin wiggled them, trying to increase their circulation.

A light flickered through the small window in the wooden door that blocked the entrance to Myrddin's cell. Myrddin shifted, awkward, the shackles digging into his wrists. A rime of blood seeped around the metal band every time he moved, the edge cutting farther into his skin. Then the door opened to reveal Modred himself and two guards, one of whom carried an upright, wooden chair. He set it in the middle of the cell. Modred turned it around and sat facing Myrddin, his arms resting along the top rail.

"So," he said. "Now that we both are situated more comfortably, perhaps you'll answer some of my questions."

It was a jest, but Myrddin wasn't laughing. "I answered truthfully before. I would have answered whatever other questions you chose to put to me in your hall."

"Perhaps." Modred flicked a crumb off his sleeve with one finger towards the rats in the corner. The rats scurried to where the crumb had fallen and after a brief scuffle, the dominant one ate it. Myrddin watched, horrified, thinking of how easily one could take a bite out of him. "But not as quickly or completely."

Myrddin moved his eyes back to Modred's face. "Why would I be any more likely to do as you ask now, since you're going to kill me anyway?"

"Ah," Modred said. "But the manner of your death remains a mystery. It is something to be negotiated."

Myrddin had known all along that Modred was a murderous son-of-a-bitch. What Welshman didn't know that? But, naïvely, Myrddin hadn't expected him to direct this level of villainy at him. Then again, this was the man who hanged a couple of hundred his own people so he could confiscate their possessions—and pay for his war against Arthur. There was nothing that wasn't beyond this man. Worse, Modred knew that Myrddin knew it.

When Myrddin didn't reply, Modred nodded at one of the guards, who fisted his hand and shot it into Myrddin's midsection. If Myrddin's bonds hadn't held him tightly, he would have gone down and stayed down. As it was, he couldn't even bend forward to better absorb the blow.

"Now," Modred said. "I want the truth. What happened at the Menai Strait?"

"I told you already." Myrddin said. "Cedric did too. It was just as he said."

The guard backhanded Myrddin across the face and his head clunked against the stones behind him. Blood formed at the corner of his mouth and dripped down his chin. Myrddin turned his head and hunched his shoulders, trying to staunch it on his shirt. He couldn't reach, however, and fell back, moaning more from frustration at his helplessness than the pain.

"I want the rest." Modred said. "There's more. What haven't you told me?"

Myrddin was at a loss, both for something else to give and for what Arthur would think was acceptable for him to say. Myrddin took a stab at a new piece of information. "We sabotaged the boats."

"Better," Modred said. "Whose idea was that?"

"Mine."

Another blow to the kidneys.

"I want the traitor's name," Modred said.

Myrddin must have looked as blank as he felt because he received another shot to the face. "Traitor? You mean Lord Cai?"

Modred's face purpled, revealing a passion that was likely to give him heart failure. In his youth, Modred had been Cai's squire. They'd remained close companions for many years afterwards, even after Modred began to assert his own claim to the throne over Cai's. Whatever bond had survived the years had been severed with Cai's latest actions. Perhaps in Modred—as in Cai—love and hatred were two sides of the same coin.

Modred and Myrddin stared at each other and slowly Modred's color subsided. He barked a laugh. "I'll give you that. He betrays both sides as it pleases him. No, I want the traitor in my ranks. The one who informed you that Wulfere would cross the Strait that day. I want to know why you were ready for him."

Myrddin opted for a shrug. "We knew. I don't know all the people who told us, but there were many sources. Wulfere was too open about his plans, at least on the Anglesey side. Not all the people there support the Saxon cause."

Another slap, which Myrddin should have known was coming for being cheeky.

"Names," Modred said.

"I have none to give you." Before Myrddin could elaborate on that lack of knowledge, he received another thrust to his abdomen. The pain was intense. His ears still rang from the previous blow and his eyes no longer saw straight. A black mist rose across his vision. Myrddin fought it, blinking and struggling to stay conscious, even though the blackness would have been a relief. "A doxy. A fisherman. A ferryman. A nun. They all told us."

Modred eased backwards. Myrddin had a brief hope that he'd leave, but Modred got to his feet and came around the chair to stand in front of Myrddin. "You can do better than that."

Myrddin tried to focus on his face, but there appeared to be several of him now. "You have two noses." He found the idea amusing, but the words came out slurred and his eyes blurred from tears he couldn't stop from falling. They hadn't even left him the dignity of wiping at them with the back of his hand.

Modred snorted his disgust. "He's done. For now." He turned away, followed by the guards who pulled the door closed behind them and left the cell in darkness.

5

14 November 537 AD

"You are well and truly out of your mind!" Ifan followed Nell down the hall towards Lord Cedric of Brecon's quarters, a stack of logs in his arms for stoking the fire in Cedric's room.

Nell glanced back at him, careful not to tip her tray of food and drink. "Am I? And what was your plan for getting Myrddin out of prison? A straight assault?"

They'd arrived at Rhuddlan in time to see Myrddin hauled away from Cedric's table—and the protest, albeit slight, that engendered from Cedric—and then spent the rest of that night and the next day mingling among the lowlier members of the castle. They both spoke Saxon, Nell better than Ifan, but only Welsh had been required so far, which had caused a slow boil in Nell's chest she was working hard to contain. Her people had done far more to betray Arthur than the Saxons ever could. Well, except for his looming death at the hands of Edgar of Wigmore.

"Better than all this sneaking around," Ifan mumbled, not so low that she couldn't hear him.

At the same time, he hadn't protested more than that, and so far had not objected to her taking charge of this aspect of the endeavor. Clearly, she'd spent far too many years in the company of women and her confidence was out of place in a castle run by men. "You got us safely to Rhuddlan," she said. "Trust me to manage this."

Ifan had caught her coming out of her room back at Garth Celyn, dressed as a boy. At first, Ifan hadn't recognized her, which was all to the good as far as she was concerned. Then he'd grabbed her arm, hissing. "What are you doing?"

"Going after Myrddin," she said.

"Alone? Are you mad?" he said. "Myrddin told me what happened at St. Asaph; what he'd arrived almost too late to stop. You'd risk that again?"

"Better than staying here and allowing him to go into danger alone," Nell had said. "To die at Modred's hands. I don't—I don't have a good feeling about this."

That had brought Ifan up short. He'd looked at her, suspicious. Nell gazed back. Unfortunately, it was no less than the truth, although as always, not all of it. Myrddin went off on his own all the time; the difference today was her dream last night. Frighteningly, instead of dreaming as

Myrddin as she always had, she'd watched the battle from above, looking down on the king's death. Myrddin wasn't even there. Nell's breath caught in her throat at what that might mean.

Even admitting that, she had to acknowledge that her visions of Arthur's death took her only so far. Sometimes she simply had a *feeling* that she should do something, or that something wasn't right—like she could sense the currents and emotions of the people around her and they all added up to a conclusion that she couldn't explain. She'd felt that way in the first moments of Wulfere's attack on her convent. To her regret, she *hadn't* felt it when she'd left her sisters alone in the barn. But she'd learned not to ignore her sense of wrongness when it came.

Ifan nodded. "Neither do I. But this is not a task for a woman. I'll go."

"No!" Nell had said. "You're not going anywhere without me."

"I'll tell the king—"

Nell cut Ifan off with a finger to his lips. "Don't you dare. Besides, I'm a free woman, with no husband or obligations to anyone but myself."

"Except to Myrddin?" Ifan had said.

"That is my choice," Nell said.

Ifan had stared into her face for a long moment, and then nodded. "I'll talk to Geraint."

So here they were, thirty miles from Garth Celyn, in the very belly of the Saxon beast. Nell raised a hand to knock at Cedric's door.

"Come in."

Nell pushed the door open and entered the room, followed by Ifan. The room was less rich than some she'd seen in the castle. She'd flitted in and out of many over the last hours, always accompanied by Ifan and his logs. Nobody had to know that those were the same three pieces of wood he'd carried all day. They'd simply moved from room to room, purposeful and diligent, determining the lay of the land. Nobody ever questioned them or wondered at their actions. Far more than at Garth Celyn, servants here were invisible—even to other servants, provided she and Ifan kept their heads down. Rhuddlan was so huge that it was impossible for any one person to keep track of all the comings and goings.

"My lord," Nell said in Saxon, curtseying, "I've brought you a meal."

Cedric glanced up. "I didn't ask for—" He cut off the sentence when Nell met his gaze with a sharp look she couldn't help. It had been far sharper than he'd probably received from anyone since he was in his nurse's care. "I see," he said, after a quick scan of her face and clothes. "Put it there."

"My name is Nell ferch Morgan," Nell said, abandoning the pretense that she was a boy. She gestured to Ifan, "and this is Ifan, from Garth Celyn."

"You're Myrddin's rescue party, are you?" Cedric said, his mind discerning the truth faster than Nell could have hoped. "Are there more of you?"

"No." Nell paused. "Unless you're willing to help us?"

"Now why would I want to do that?"

Nell gazed at him, her expression calm while she thought furiously for an answer.

But it was Ifan who spoke. "Because you've got bigger *ceilliau* than Modred."

Cedric smiled.

* * * * *

"We're getting you out of here," Nell said.

Myrddin swam upwards towards the faint light in his cell, coming to himself with his arms around Nell and his head on her shoulder.

"You," he said, feeling marvelous all of a sudden.

Ifan crouched at Myrddin's feet, working at the chains that bound his ankles. Myrddin imagined they too were blood-rimmed, but his lower extremities were so numb from the cold and being forced to stay in one position for so long, he couldn't feel them.

A voice growled from behind Nell. "*I'm* getting you out of here."

Myrddin lifted his head to squint towards the form in the doorway.

Cedric lounged against the frame, his arms folded across his chest. "Hurry up. We haven't much time."

"Not like his lordship couldn't help," Ifan muttered in Welsh, under his breath.

"I grew up in Wales," Cedric said, his voice mild. "I learned Welsh in my nurse's arms."

Nell lifted a hand to Myrddin's face. With shaking fingers, she touched his eyebrow. "It's the only part of you that isn't wounded." She was trying to jest, but her voice wavered.

At last Ifan fitted the key into the final lock and opened it. "We need to move."

"I'm fine." Myrddin took a step. "Let's get out of here."

Just because the manacles were loose, however, didn't mean he could walk. If Nell hadn't still been holding him, he would have fallen. Seeing Myrddin's peril, Ifan came up on his other side, his arm around Myrddin's waist. Together, they hobbled towards the door, Myrddin's feet tingling as the blood rushed into them. Myrddin feared for guards, but Cedric kept a smirk on his face, unconcerned about the treasonous act in which he was openly participating. He turned at their approach, led the way across the stones of the foyer where Myrddin had seen guards earlier, and up the stairs.

They came out of the stairwell into a larger room containing three soldiers, all unconscious. One sprawled across the table at which he'd been sitting at dice, while his companion's head lolled against the right hand wall. The third guard had fallen off his bench onto the floor. He lay on his side, legs splayed in front of him. Like the others, his eyes were closed.

"Drunk." Cedric strode past the table at which they sat, not looking at them but at the same time not even attempting to be quiet.

"The poppy juice I brought helped," Nell said.

Myrddin swiveled his head, searching for his weapons, but Ifan had taken care of the problem. "Your sword's right here." He patted his waist. "We recovered it first, in case we had to leave in a hurry. I left mine outside the castle with the horses."

"Thank you," Myrddin said, the sound coming out more as a grunt than a word.

A moment later, they were through the far doorway and into the outer bailey. The dungeon—or at least Myrddin's dungeon—was situated in the basement of the southwest, square, guard tower that overlooked the Clwyd River. The guardroom door sat at the base of the tower wall, effectively in a ditch, looking up to the inner wall, over two hundred feet away. If Modred had held Myrddin in one of the six towers that defended the inner bailey, he'd never have escaped.

Myrddin had known where Modred had put him, of course, and now that he was being rescued, it seemed more suspicious than lucky to be so far from the central workings of the castle. Then again, maybe Modred didn't like to disturb the castle inhabitants, including his beloved wife, with screaming. Cedric led them along the curtain wall that fronted the river to the river gate. The drawbridge was up, as it had been when Myrddin had arrived, but the postern door was unguarded. As Cedric drew it open, a moan sounded from farther along the wall in the shadow of the tower.

"He sent him a whore." Nell whispered to Myrddin as she and Ifan dragged Myrddin through the opening.

Cedric didn't come with them. "I leave you here." He halted in the doorway. "You may retrieve your horse at Brecon Castle, my home, should you care to do so."

Myrddin pulled his right arm over Nell's head and held it out to Cedric. "Thank you."

Cedric grasped Myrddin's forearm, nodded stiffly, and shut the door in Myrddin's face. He'd gone before Myrddin realized he'd never responded to Arthur's message.

But then, on second thought, perhaps he had.

Nell, Ifan, and Myrddin staggered down the sharp bank that descended from the postern gate to the river. They could have crossed at a low spot half a mile upstream, but it wouldn't do to walk under the walls and expose themselves on the castle side of the Clywd, even at this hour of the night. The sooner they left the vicinity of Rhuddlan the better.

"Can you swim?" Nell said.

"He's a fish when his arms work," Ifan said.

"I'm here," Myrddin said. "I can speak."

"In," Nell said.

Obediently, Myrddin plunged into the water and struck out for the opposite bank. At worst, if he couldn't have made it, he could have let the current carry him north to the ford that he'd ridden across on Cadfarch. Determined to succeed and not put Ifan or Nell into any further danger, Myrddin forced himself to stroke and kick long enough to reach the muddy bank. He crawled up it, bedraggled and soaking wet, although the cold water made his wounds feel a bit better. Myrddin could even sense his feet and for the first time was happy not to have worn boots. Nell and Ifan had kept theirs on and would have to stop once they were clear of the castle to empty them of water.

"How far?" Myrddin said, once they'd clawed their way out of the brush, onto the road, and then across it into the ditch on the other side.

"We left the horses close by." Nell grasped Myrddin's arm and lifted him out of the scrub. "You can make it."

"I'm not sure that I can do anything anymore without you." The words were out before he could censor them. Nell had her head up, watching the road, and didn't respond, for which Myrddin was grateful. Perhaps she hadn't heard him.

'Close by' wasn't quite as close as he'd hoped. More time passed, Myrddin hobbling on tender feet, before they reached the copse of beech trees in which Ifan had tied the horses. They'd only brought two, so once again, Nell and Myrddin would share. Ifan passed Myrddin his water flask but Myrddin's hands were so cold and he was so tired, he couldn't remove the stopper. Nell pulled it out, but even then, his hands shook so much that the water spilled out the top. In the end, Nell placed both of her hands on either side of his and helped Myrddin tip it up. Then she had to help him out of his wet clothes and into loose breeches and shirt.

"From Caerhun again?" he said as she fastened the cloak around his neck.

"Rhodri laughed when I asked for them," she said, "but gave way. It was better to be safe than sorry."

Finally, when they were all dressed, Myrddin had to face the notion of climbing on the horse. The saddle looked miles away.

"Come on, lad," Ifan said.

Myrddin rested a hand on Nell's shoulder while Ifan steadied him. With his foot in a stirrup, they shoved Myrddin hard upwards, shooting him towards the saddle. He sprawled across the horse's withers, exhausted. With some more pushing from Ifan, Myrddin managed to swing his leg over the horse's back and straighten. His forearm was one of the few limbs that didn't hurt, so Myrddin offered it to Nell. She grasped it, clambering into place behind him.

Every bone, muscle, and nerve in Myrddin's body screamed at him. The only reason he was even upright was because Nell held him on the horse. It had been a long time since he'd felt this terrible. If it wouldn't end up hurting him more, Myrddin would have rubbed his face to hide the tears—of pain and the frustration that he couldn't control—that threatened to spill from his eyes.

Myrddin swallowed hard. "Talk," he said, once they urged the horses out of the brush and had given them their heads.

"We followed you," Ifan said, giving Myrddin a chance to gather his wits. "I got permission from Lord Geraint—more or less—and we were gone within an hour of your own departure. As we knew where you were going, we hardly needed to trail you closely."

"Where'd you get the boys' clothes?" Myrddin asked Nell.

"From a stable boy," she said. "He'd outgrown them and his mother'd been saving them for his younger brother."

"And then?" Myrddin said, when neither wanted to continue.

"We followed you all the way here." Ifan shrugged.

"There was a chance you'd rest with the garrison at Caerhun," Nell said, "but Rhodri said they hadn't seen you."

"Or rather," Ifan added, "they'd seen you but you'd crossed the ford instead of turning in at the fort."

"Because we took time at Caerhun and had to hide the horses, we reached Rhuddlan a few hours behind you. It was full dark, but the villagers were still up and about."

"We entered the castle in the back of a hay wagon," Ifan said.

The tag-team story telling was giving Myrddin a headache, but they were in full spate and Myrddin chose not to stop them. "Go on."

"Hundreds of people work in that castle," Ifan said. "As I left my weapons and armor with the horses on the other side of the Clywd, it was a simple matter to pretend to be other than what we are."

"What I want to know, more than anything, is about Cedric," Myrddin said. "How did you convince him to free me?"

"That was my idea," Nell said. "We dined in the hall at the same time you did—after you'd met with Modred. To our eyes, Cedric didn't object to your company; although we didn't know how you'd met, it seemed fortuitous, given the discussion you and I had at Garth Celyn."

"So when the guards hauled you away," Ifan said, "and Cedric protested, albeit not loudly and not to Modred, we decided to take a chance on him."

"What did you do? Walk up to him and say, 'Greetings. We're with Myrddin. Will you help us free him from the dungeon?'"

Ifan laughed from deep in his chest. "Yes. If I'm ever in a tight place, I'd prefer to have Nell with me. She was as bold as Queen Gwenhwyfar herself."

"He deliberated only briefly before he agreed to help you escape," Nell said. "We watched for Modred to come to you again, but he didn't. He went to his bed and then we acted."

"Thank you for freeing me." Myrddin realized he hadn't yet said it. "It was quite a chance you took."

"I hope Cedric doesn't suffer for it," Nell said, "once Modred realizes you're gone."

The crisp air, along with their story, had perked Myrddin up considerably, even as his muscles stiffened from the cold. "He's Cedric ap Aelfric. He gave the guards wine and women, and if they remember what passed in the night, it will be a miracle. When Cedric tells Modred that he had nothing to do with my escape, if it even comes to that, it will be good enough for Modred."

"Cedric said he wouldn't leave Rhuddlan until the guards discovered your absence, after which he and his men would travel south to Brecon." Ifan paused, thinking. "I'm missing something, aren't I?"

"As in, the why of it? Why did he risk his own neck to free me?" The sight of Cedric in the doorway was fresh in

Myrddin's mind and he felt a weight lifting from his shoulders. "He is willing to consider an alliance with King Arthur."

"He said that?" Nell said.

"He showed it," Myrddin said.

6

"Can you hear me, Myrddin?" Nell leaned over Myrddin's inert form.

Although Myrddin didn't reply, he did open his eyes to look into her face. The room was dark, except for a candle on the table at the foot of the pallet on which he lay. Nell smiled, even though it cost her. Myrddin didn't smile back, just stared, unseeing, and then let his eyes close. Nell stroked his cheek with one finger. And then she did smile, albeit mockingly, at what he'd think when he discovered that she'd shaved his mustache in order to tend to the gash above his lip.

It had been a long, grim ride from Rhuddlan Castle. Myrddin had been so much weaker than usual and the last few miles had almost been his undoing. It had been all she could do to hold him on the horse. Modred's men had wounded him inside and out, though she wouldn't know how bad the damage was inside him until the rest of him began to heal.

"Would you like to hear a story?" she said.

Again, Myrddin didn't answer. He'd squeezed the hand she was holding earlier, but now his grip softened. She gazed down at his closed eyes, thinking of what story to tell, and whether it was time to tell him a true one. "Once upon a time, there was a little girl …

She was just like any other little girl—shocking red hair, green eyes, pointed chin—doted upon by her father, especially as he'd lost his wife at her birth.

One day, as she was wandering in the trees along the river near her home, looking for any winter herbs that had survived the snow, she heard voices—men's voices—very close. They shouted at one another. Hooves pounded on the soft earth and then not ten feet from her, a company of five men wearing King Arthur's crest rode out of the woods, swords and shields raised high. They splashed through the water and up the bank on the other side.

The girl was frightened. She ran the opposite way, but instead of running into her father's field as she expected, she found herself in a clearing, next to a church. All around her men called and horses neighed. She ran for the entrance to the church, but just as she reached it, the door opened. A man appeared, older than her father, his dark hair shot with grey. She'd never seen him before, but somehow she knew he was their king. He pulled his sword from his sheath, shouted at the men behind him, and retreated back inside.

Oddly, the man didn't see her. A moment later, the men who'd ridden through the water returned, racing their horses towards a line of Saxon soldiers that had burst from the woods on the other side of the clearing. All around her men fought and died.

Then, one man in particular caught her attention. He'd lost his helmet and his black hair had come loose. His shield was gone too and between forcing his sword through a Saxon's belly and turning to race for the front of the church, he thrust his hair out of his face with his free hand.

In that space of time, she caught his eye. They stared at each other. They couldn't have been more different: her, small, scrawny, not yet blooming into womanhood; and him, a tall, dark-haired soldier, older, with lines around his eyes.

Then he broke away, racing to defend his king. She watched him barrel into a Saxon soldier; she watched him fall. She watched the Saxon soldiers celebrate their victory.

And it was she who pulled the man to the side, off of the body of his king whose head the Saxons soldiers had taken while they left the rest of him to rot. And it was she who wept over his grave ...

* * * * *

"So now you've saved *me*," Myrddin said. From the way the light reflected from the hallway through the open door, it was late afternoon. He'd slept a long time.

"Does that make us even?" Nell said.

"Do you want it to?"

She smiled and didn't answer, looking down at her hands. She'd tucked her hair into her cloak, but the end of her thick braid peeked from underneath the hood. Then she looked up. "It hurts me to see you this way."

"It hurts me too," he said, trying to make light of it.

"I wish we could have gotten to you sooner."

"I'll heal," he said.

"Hidden away in my convent, I forgot the horror one man could do to another," she said. "I've been reminded almost daily since then."

"Believe me, Modred is capable of much worse."

Nell nodded. "I stitched the back of your head while you were asleep. I kept waiting for you to wake in the middle of it and argue with me about the proper method." She smiled, and then added, "I would have had Ifan cosh you to put you back to sleep."

Myrddin laughed and then tried to suppress it, moving his hand to his chest. "Don't!" He swallowed the mirth and the pain the laughter had caused. "Where's Ifan now?"

"He stayed up with you most of the night," she said. "Did you know *he's* in pain nearly all the time?"

"It's his back," Myrddin said. "He injured it ten years ago—doing less than nothing, mind you—and it's never been the same since. But a soldier who can't ride and fight isn't a soldier anymore."

"I told him I'd make a rubbing salve for him when we returned to Garth Celyn." She turned her head to look through the doorway. The scent of greenery and outside air wafted through it, indicating that the temperature had risen. "It's peaceful here, isn't it? I didn't notice the first time we came through."

"We're at Caerhun?" Myrddin said.

Nell nodded. "That was the longest twenty miles I've ever ridden."

Footsteps sounded along the corridor. "You're awake." Rhodri poked his head through the doorway.

"In a manner of speaking," Myrddin said. "Thank you for your hospitality, as before."

"I thought you'd like to know that the Saxons patrol the eastern bank of the river. Three separate companies have ridden to the ford, to turn around at the water's edge. I would not have said you were that valuable." A grin split Rhodri's face.

"Nor I," Myrddin said.

Rhodri shrugged. "Let me know if you need anything, miss," he said to Nell.

"Thank you."

Rhodri left.

Myrddin gazed up at the ceiling, thinking about the past and the future and all that lay between them. He didn't fear death. He hadn't for many years, not with living it every night in his dreams. But despair was as close a companion for him over the years as for Nell, and it had overwhelmed him after Modred had left the dungeon. To have come so close to making a difference in whether Arthur lived or died, only to die at Modred's hand, had left him bereft. Now that they'd fled the castle and were safe in Arthur's lands again, the emotions he'd been holding in check came flooding back.

"I should have guessed that you were up to something," Myrddin said. "When I turned to look back at the castle and saw you and Ifan on the battlements, I should have been suspicious. Had you already decided what you were going to do?"

"I'd already decided to come after you, but Ifan wouldn't let me come alone."

"I should hope not," Myrddin said. "Were you afraid?"

"Not during the journey; not even when we reached the crossroads at St. Asaph. Ifan is a strong swordsman or you wouldn't trust him. I was afraid for you; that Modred had already murdered you before we reached Rhuddlan."

"I was afraid of that too," Myrddin said.

"The only comfort," Nell said, "was the assumption that you knew what you were doing."

Myrddin started to laugh and then swallowed it, trying not to move. "I'm not so sure you should have relied on that notion."

Nell smiled. "Once Cedric said he'd assist us, however, things moved quickly and I hardly had time to think. He had it all in hand."

"Thank you," Myrddin said. "I don't know that Cedric would have freed me unless you encouraged him."

"I'm not so sure," Nell said. "It would depend on how much he thought he could gain from sticking his neck out."

"He stuck it pretty far," Myrddin said.

"He did," Nell said. "What did you say to him to make the two of you so friendly?"

"I told him that Arthur wanted to negotiate—to talk to him—even to work out an alliance."

Myrddin had closed his eyes again, as keeping them open was just too much work, but at Nell's silence, turned his head to look at her. A range of emotions crossed her face: shock, disbelief, puzzlement, and then understanding.

"Given that the king has never said any such thing, you took a risk," she said. "Suppose King Arthur doesn't want to talk to him?"

"Why wouldn't he? The king is willing to talk to Edgar, and he's far less likely a turncoat than Cedric. Cedric, at least, has a history of rebellion. Edgar is the son of the only Saxon lord with interests in Wales never to waver in Modred's cause, for all Modred has angered him now."

"What are you going to tell King Arthur?"

"The truth," Myrddin said. "Even your part of it—provided you do not object?" He studied her face. She had a smudge on her nose and a second along one cheek.

Nell lifted her hands and dropped them in an expression of resignation and helplessness. "Ifan and I made our choice. I don't regret it. Given that we rescued you, I'd hope King Arthur wouldn't either."

Myrddin nodded. "I'm glad you've told me everything now," he said. "I'm glad you know that you can trust me."

Nell sat silent for a long count of ten. "You weren't asleep."

"No."

Nell stayed frozen, her legs in front of her and her back against the wall.

"You have visions," Myrddin said, not as a question. "You've had them of me."

Nell swallowed hard. "Since I was a girl."

"Back at Garth Celyn you cried my name in the night. You've done so often in the nights that followed."

"You've haunted me all my life," she said. "The story I told you was a waking dream—my first and only. It's why I've always known that you were real, even when all I had were dreams."

Myrddin nodded.

"You're not upset by this." Nell canted her head to one side and looking at him curiously. "Why aren't you afraid of me? Or at the very least, suspicious?"

"On December 11th, a month from now, if we do not stop it, King Arthur will die at the hands of a Saxon soldier, near a church by the Cam River," Myrddin said.

"That's what I see in my dreams," Nell said. "I just told you that story last night. That's what I dream nearly every night now. It's changed a bit in the last few days. But—"

Myrddin interrupted. "That's *my* dream, ever since I was twelve years old."

The relief he felt in admitting it to Nell—and that she would understand everything he felt—filled him. His was a true seeing and they'd been given this vision for a reason. It appeared to be *their* job—his and Nell's—by what means he didn't know and couldn't imagine from where he lay—to ensure that his king did not meet Edgar by the Cam. He met Nell's eyes as understanding entered them: *their* vision; *their* task; *their* destiny.

Nell stared at him. "It's not just me, then!"

Myrddin shook his head. "It's not just you."

7

16 November 537 AD

Myrddin slept again, woke in the early evening, and then slept in fits and starts throughout a second night at Caerhun. Every time he tried to roll over, he awoke in pain, but either Ifan or Nell was there to ease him into a more comfortable position. Ifan had a soldier's ability to watch or sleep in whatever situation he found himself, but the times Nell sat beside him, she talked. Some of what she said Myrddin remembered, but mostly he let the sound of her voice wash over him as she related a story from her girlhood, or another from the tales of the *Dôn*. She didn't speak of the dreams again, but then, Myrddin knew that story too well himself.

At dawn, Myrddin came to himself enough to realize that he couldn't delay any longer and neither Nell nor Ifan protested that they should stay. They knew as well as he that King Arthur awaited word of Myrddin's journey. Soon, the king would begin to fear that Myrddin would never return. Most importantly, Myrddin had information for him and Myrddin didn't want him doing anything rash because of lack of knowledge.

In the pouring rain, which was a match to the companions' low mood, they made their slow way out of Caerhun. By late afternoon, they had reached the last stretch, descending down the road from the standing stones to Garth Celyn; the men-at-arms on the battlements saw them coming and opened the gates, welcoming them home. In the muddy bailey, Nell slid off the horse. Myrddin climbed down with Ifan's help, his body stiff and a hand at his ribs. Even though they'd walked the horses the whole way, Myrddin could barely move from the effort the journey had cost him. Most of the day was gone, as slow as they'd taken it.

"Your face looks much worse." It came out as a matter-of-fact comment as Nell steered him towards the hall. "I have something inside to help with the bruising."

"It's my ribs that ache the most," Myrddin said. "I'm glad Modred's lackeys didn't puncture a lung."

"From my examination, all your bones are whole," she said. "Not to diminish the pain, but I felt you all over when you were unconscious and you're only bruised."

"*Only*," Myrddin said.

Nell tsked through her teeth. "Infant."

They'd taken one step up the stairs to the double doors that guarded the hall when one of the doors opened to reveal King Arthur. Nell and Myrddin froze, their heads tipped up, looking into his face. He pursed his lips; then took two steps down to where they stood. Without saying anything, either admonishment or praise, he placed Myrddin's arm over his shoulder. Taking most of the weight off Nell, he hobbled with Myrddin into the hall, across it, and down the corridor.

"I need to rest." Myrddin's breath came in gasps.

"In here." Arthur maneuvered him through the door to his receiving room and onto his own padded chair. He motioned to Nell to shut the door behind them. "Better to talk in private."

The room contained two more men: Bedwyr, as always, since he never left King Arthur's side while he was at Garth Celyn except to sleep, and a much younger man standing with him, a youth, no more than sixteen or seventeen, albeit full grown—tall and well built—with shoulders used to wearing armor. Arthur straightened as Myrddin collapsed into the chair and Nell put a hand to his upper arm to keep him from falling out of it.

Not giving Myrddin a chance to catch his breath, King Arthur held out a hand to the boy, who took a step closer. "Myrddin."

Myrddin looked up. Arthur's tone had been abrupt, but now an uncharacteristic smile—one Myrddin might even call gleeful—covered his face.

"Meet Huw ap Myrddin. Your son."

The boy looked straight at Myrddin, staring with an unrelieved intensity, and gave Myrddin a slight and very stiff bow. "Father."

"Wha—" Myrddin gaped at the boy, his head empty of any thought with which to work. "Who?"

"Huw ap Myrddin." The boy's spine matched his words, taut, like a bow string set to loose its arrow.

Myrddin's eyes ranged from the top of the boy's head to his boots, stunned speechless.

"My mother was Tegwan. From Brecon," Huw said, still quivering.

Tegwan. Dear God. He stared at the boy, this unexpected gift, and managed a nod. He remembered her—if the vague image of shape and form could be called a memory. Then Myrddin caught Huw's choice of words. "Was?" he said. "She *was* called Tegwan?"

"My mother died two months ago," Huw said. "I've been looking for you ever since."

"I do remember her," Myrddin said, not exactly lying.

Huw released a long breath and his shoulders sagged.

It was as if Myrddin had passed a test he hadn't known he was taking. If he'd had the strength to pace, he would have, but as it was, Myrddin shifted in his chair, hot and uncomfortable. "She never told me about you. I would have acknowledged you as my son had I known you existed. Surely Tegwan knew that?"

"My mother married someone else." Then Huw paused, swallowed hard, and continued, "A Saxon. He knew I wasn't his son because she was already pregnant by the time they married, but he preferred to say I was his. I grew up thinking that he was my natural father. They had no other children and when my father died two years ago, my mother told me the truth."

Myrddin waited for more. He could hardly accuse Huw of neglecting to search for him sooner, given that Huw knew nothing of Myrddin or where he was. And he'd been raised half-Saxon. That wasn't easily put aside.

"My mother was ill herself by then, a wasting disease, and I couldn't leave her beyond my regular duties to my lord," Huw said. "I came north to Gwynedd as soon as he gave me leave to find you."

"And who is your lord?" Myrddin said.

Huw bit his lip and glanced at Arthur, who nodded. Huw hemmed and hawed for another few seconds, and then blurted it out. "Lord Cedric of Brecon."

"Ho!" Nell said from beside Myrddin. "Well, that's a tangle, isn't it?"

"Did you tell him my name?" Myrddin said. "And that I served King Arthur?"

"Of course," Huw said. "For what it was worth, as you go only by your first name. My lord Cedric had less need of me during these few weeks of the Archbishop's truce. He didn't want me to come with him to Anglesey so he gave me permission to search for you."

And to act as his spy in the Welsh camp? The thought rose unbidden, but once admitted, couldn't be ignored. Myrddin looked at the king. "It was Cedric, with Nell and Ifan's assistance, who freed me from the Rhuddlan dungeon."

"Did he now?" Arthur scanned Myrddin's wounded body. It was impossible to hide the damage to his face or the awkward and uncomfortable way in which he was sitting.

Every square inch of him, hurt, except perhaps his eyebrow, as Nell had noted.

Huw, too, perked up at the mention of his patron's name. "My lord freed you? But who did this?" Uncertainty entered his eyes for the first time. "Surely not Modred!"

"Surely it was Modred," Myrddin said. "Or rather, Modred's guards on his behalf."

"Tell me that Lord Cedric wasn't present at the time!"

"He was not," Myrddin said. "I spoke with him at length earlier in the evening. We were dining together when the guards took me away."

"I have always found Lord Cedric to be fair and honorable," Huw said.

"We know." Myrddin flapped a hand in his direction and managed not to laugh at him openly. "Stand down."

Arthur turned to Nell. "Perhaps you could find our young man some food and drink."

"Yes, my lord." Nell straightened and released Myrddin's hand, which she'd been holding tightly. Myrddin nodded at Huw and hoped that Nell understood that it was not she who was being dismissed, but Huw.

The boy came forward. As he reached Myrddin's chair, Myrddin held out a hand to stop him. "Wait." With one hand on the table in front of him for support, he got to his feet so he could stand face to face with his son. They possessed similar coloring and were of a height, although Huw was perhaps a half inch taller. The boy had Myrddin's straight nose but his mother's blue eyes, where Myrddin's were hazel. Myrddin settled a hand on each of Huw's shoulders and gripped them. "I'm glad you came to find me. Any man would be proud to claim you as his son."

Huw held Myrddin's arms, his fingers tight around his biceps. "Thank you, sir." He still carried himself with a tenseness that kept his shoulders back and his jaw firm, but some of the anxiety seemed to have left him.

"Nell is a good friend," Myrddin said. "She'll take care of you."

"Yes, Father." With a last, direct look, Huw left the room with Nell.

Myrddin sank back into his seat, his head in his hands. King Arthur, having lost his usual chair to Myrddin, perched on the edge of the desk. Bedwyr found a seat on the bench under the window.

"I'd be delighted to know what's going on," King Arthur said.

Myrddin looked up. "Damned if I know, my lord. Huw—" Myrddin made a helpless gesture towards the door. "I didn't know."

Bedwyr spoke from his corner. "Didn't your mother neglect to divulge the identity of *your* father before she died?"

"Yes," Myrddin said. "At least Tegwan gave the boy my name and encouraged him to find me, once her husband was dead."

"What was your mother's name again?" Bedwyr said.

Myrddin glanced at him, not sure why he wanted to know. "I don't know that I've ever told you. Her name was Seren ferch Gruffydd."

"An unusual name, Seren," Bedwyr said.

"Did you know her?" Myrddin checked Bedwyr's face again, which he was always careful to keep blank. Lord Cedric could take lessons from him.

"I never met her," Bedwyr said.

Myrddin nodded and clutched at his hair. Arthur had risen from the table while Bedwyr and Myrddin talked, and now moved to stand at the window, looking out at the flickering lights of the torches in the bailey, his hands clasped behind his back. "I did."

Myrddin's jaw dropped.

"Her father was an ally of mine until he defected to King Icel of Mercia the year before my uncle died. His action left his daughter alone, here at Garth Celyn, as one of my Aunt Juliana's ladies."

Towards the end of the 490's, King Icel of Mercia had appeared unstoppable. He'd wooed many a Welsh lord away from Ambrosius with promises of land and power, were he to conquer Wales once and for all. Instead, King Ambrosius and Arthur had defeated the allied Saxon forces in the summer of 500 AD at Mt. Badon. Unfortunately, Ambrosius had died in February of 501, followed six months later by Arthur's father, Uther. This left a gap in authority, filled instantly—if inadequately—by Arthur himself, then aged twenty-one.

Myrddin had been born into Madoc's household in September of 501—into a year of upheaval and strife. Each of the remaining Welsh lords, along with all of the Saxon barons, saw themselves as possible heirs to Ambrosius' throne. They'd fought among themselves for control of Wales. Though it was Arthur, of course, who triumphed. It was to avoid that horror again that many Welsh lords supported Modred now, preferring an orderly transition to possible war.

"I didn't know that," Myrddin said. "I thought my mother had grown up in Madoc's charge."

"No."

"But—"

"Speak to me of Cedric," King Arthur said.

Myrddin blinked, not wanting to leave the subject of his mother, but unable to disobey. "I don't know if you're going to like what I have to say, my lord. I took some liberties ..."

"And paid for them, by the looks." Bedwyr's lips curved into a smile.

Myrddin coughed and laughed at the same time. "You could say that. Although as I told you before, these wounds were courtesy of Modred." Myrddin took a deep breath, his abdomen aching at the effort. "After I gave Modred your letter, he directed me to bring Lord Cedric of Brecon to him. Thus, Cedric and I had a few moments of privacy in his room. I took the opportunity to suggest that you, my lord, would be open to a discussion of the disposition of various lands in Wales, if Cedric reconsidered his allegiance."

King Arthur swung around to stare at Myrddin.

"I apologize, my lord," Myrddin said. "It seemed like a good idea at the time, and the odds of him agreeing, or of anything coming of it at all, seemed worth the slight risk to my neck."

"It was obviously worth far more than that to Cedric," Bedwyr said. "And the fact that he had already heard your name from Huw sheds new light on the entire matter."

"It does," Myrddin said, although he was having a hard time figuring out what exactly it told him. He was feeling more and more wobbly and desperately wanted a drink, a bed, and Nell's gentle hand on his forehead, not necessarily in that order. "One more thing. Modred knows that you've sent Lord Gawain to Powys to marshal men against the Saxon lords there. Worse, Cedric told him of Edgar of Wigmore's letter to you. I don't know how he knew of it, except if Edgar himself told him."

The two men observed Myrddin, unspeaking, too well-practiced at absorbing bad news to show it openly, but clearly nonplussed. Bedwyr put down his cup of wine and leaned forward. "Go on."

"They are convinced, both of them, that Edgar is not sincere in his desire to ally with you and intends to lure you into an ambush, my lord king," Myrddin said, and then ventured to assert his own opinion. "I would think that likely."

"Thank you, Myrddin," Bedwyr said, implying he wasn't at all thankful for his advice, and then continued, half under his breath to the king—"The uncertainty in the air reminds me of the days after your uncle and father died, before you fully grasped the reins of Wales, my lord."

"Go to your son." King Arthur's expression softened at Myrddin's evident distress. He nodded his head towards the door. "I don't want to see you in the hall tomorrow."

"And watch Huw closely," Bedwyr said.

Myrddin looked up, dismayed at the warning in Bedwyr's tone—and yet understanding it, for he'd had the same uncomfortable thought.

"He is Cedric's man," Bedwyr said. "He's already seen too much. I would be wary of allowing him to return to Brecon."

"Yes, sir." Myrddin didn't like his observation but knew he was right. He also didn't want the presence of his son to jeopardize Arthur's new found trust in Myrddin himself.

Still, Myrddin didn't move. His head felt like it weighed fifty pounds. Before he knew it, Arthur and Bedwyr were on either side of him. They pulled him up, just as the guards had done in the hall at Rhuddlan, but more gently, and half-dragged, half-carried him down the hall, out the door and across the courtyard to the sleeping quarters in the guest house. The small closet space in which Nell and Myrddin had slept before was vacant. The pallets lay on the floor, beckoning Myrddin with their softness and warmth. He reached an arm towards one. Bedwyr and Arthur laid him down.

"I'll find Nell," Bedwyr said.

It seemed Myrddin nodded agreement, but he couldn't be sure because a second later, he was asleep.

8

17 November 537 AD

"Myrddin, damn it, get over here!"

"Coming, sir!" I hurried towards Gawain, my boots slipping in the snow, and we met in the center of the clearing by the church. In the growing darkness, the temperature had dropped and snowflakes had begun to drift down from the sky, filling in our footprints. I would have been happier to have had four more eyes in order to see in all directions. The Saxons were coming. I sure as hell wanted to be ready when they did.

"The king is inside, waiting, but I'm impatient with Edgar. I expected him here by now," Gawain said. "I think we need to leave this place."

"Yes, sir," I said. "I'll tell King Arthur."

I strode towards the door to the church, glad that Gawain had decided to follow his instincts. I reached the bottom step and was just beginning to mount the stairs *when the world blew apart. An arrow whipped by my left ear. I ducked and spun around, my sword in my hand.*

"The king! The king!"

T he first time Myrddin woke, Huw sat beside his pallet. A low candle guttered in a dish on the floor, the light flickering and reflecting off the walls of the room. Someone—Nell, perhaps—had removed his boots and covered him with a wool blanket or three; Myrddin was warm enough, even if his nose was cold since the room was one of the few in the manor house without a fireplace. He rolled onto his back, noting that someone had also taken his cloak. He spared a thought for his armor, left behind at Rhuddlan, and reconciled himself to the knowledge that it was gone forever. He trusted that Arthur would see him properly protected when it came to it again.

Pushing aside the changing dream and what it meant, Myrddin turned his head to study his son. Huw sat upright against the wall, his eyes closed. At Myrddin's movement, Huw opened them.

"Hello, Father." He didn't appear to mind saying it; Myrddin certainly wouldn't ever grow tired of hearing it. He still couldn't believe that Huw could be his.

"What is the hour?" Myrddin said.

"The chapel rang Matins not long ago," Huw said. "Your friend, Nell, said she'd relieve me at Lauds."

"You don't have to stay."

Huw shrugged. "After the events of the day, I doubt I could sleep anyway." He smiled. "It's an honor to watch over you."

His obvious admiration—a sharp contrast to his earlier near-hostility—confused Myrddin, until he considered a possible source. "Someone's been talking."

"You have many friends," Huw said. "Ifan, certainly, but Lord Geraint joined us for the evening meal. They spoke of you at length."

"Do *not* believe everything they say."

Huw laughed. "Ifan said you'd say that."

"He was there when your mother and I met. Did he speak of it?" Myrddin said.

"Only that you were a squire in King Arthur's company. You came to Brecon in the fall of 520," Huw said. "But I knew that already from my mother."

"I was nineteen. Older than you, but in no way ready to be a father." He looked at Huw. "Your mother must have known it."

"I believe she did, else, why keep you a secret? It's not as if you ever came looking for her again."

Christ. What do I say to that? "I did love her. I was careless with my heart and hers."

"And that's your excuse?" Huw's voice rose and the admiration of a moment ago was forgotten in favor of long-suppressed resentment.

"Is that why you came to find me?" Myrddin said. "To accuse me of abandoning your mother? Of abandoning you?"

Huw looked down at his hands, clenched in his lap so tightly his knuckles whitened. Then he relaxed them, smoothing the palms on the fabric of his breeches. "Yes. My anger just now caught me unawares, but I've felt it ever since my mother told me the truth."

"I served my king," Myrddin said. "I was with your mother in the fall and winter but even with the upheaval in Brecon the following year, King Arthur never called me south of Buellt again. It's my fault that I never asked leave to go." He paused, hesitating. The real truth shamed him; yet, at this late date, it was a truth from which he should not hide and which his son deserved. "And I'd not asked to go because I was afraid to see your mother—I was afraid that she would ask for a commitment from me which I felt unable to give."

"Did you ever think of her?" Huw's voice didn't reveal anger now so much as pain.

"I was a coward, Huw," Myrddin said. "The longer I waited to see her, the worse the guilt. And after a year or two, I told myself that your mother would have forgotten me; that it was better for both of us if I didn't return." Huw didn't answer straight away and then Myrddin added, his voice as gentle as he could make it, "For all that our acquaintance was short, your mother and I enjoyed each other's company."

"My mother said as much to me."

"But she still never wanted you to know about me."

Huw shifted, discomfited. Myrddin sensed he'd only added to his questions. "My father's family has served Lord Cedric for many years. My—" he licked his lips, "—father was a knight to his grandfather." He paused and glanced at Myrddin, a rueful smile on his face.

"Go on," Myrddin said. "I know the history."

"After Badon, Lord Cedric's family lost Brecon to King Arthur, but not their interest in it. My step-father was often in the area," Huw said. "He'd had his eye on my mother for some time. She was with you, and then she was with him. She wouldn't tell me more than that."

Myrddin sighed, not even remembering the nineteen-year-old he'd been. It was so long ago, he had to wade through misty memory to catch a glimpse of those long ago battles. All Myrddin truly remembered of Tegwan was the hint of a laugh when he touched her, and his own eagerness.

"I was a fool to let her go." Myrddin noted the sturdy lankiness of his son and knowing how different all their lives would have been if he'd had as much courage in his personal life as on the battlefield.

"I loved my father—my mother's husband, but I've always been half-Welsh." Huw turned his head to look at Myrddin, his face intent. "I have resented you, it's true, but it is my hope that I will no longer have to be torn in two."

Myrddin had been a father to Huw for half a day and already he needed counseling. Myrddin didn't know that he was the right one to give it, but as he was the only one available, he had no choice. "Help me to sit up."

Huw grasped Myrddin's hand and hauled him to a sitting position. Myrddin swung his legs over the edge of the pallet so he could rest next to Huw, their backs to the wall. Myrddin reached for the water cup and took a long drink.

"The world is not divided as simply as the lines between countries make us think." Myrddin set down the cup. "You are full Welsh, by blood, but you were raised by a Saxon."

"Yes," Huw said.

"A man who loved you."

"Yes." Huw paused and Myrddin let him say what he was feeling, not at all offended. "And I loved him."

"I'm glad," Myrddin said. "If I wasn't a father to you all these years, I would much rather you had a different father, than none at all."

"Was that how it was for you? You have no paternal name; you are just Myrddin."

"My mother took the name of my father to her grave," Myrddin said. "Apparently, she never told him either—or he was dead too, before my birth."

"That must have been hard."

Myrddin was a bit surprised that Huw would speak to him of it. "It certainly made it difficult to dress me down as my betters would have liked." Myrddin smiled. "Nobody could say, *Myrddin ap Geraint ap Bedwyr, get over here!*" As Myrddin hoped, Huw smiled too. "I was not unique, certainly. Many of my companions growing up had lost their fathers early in life."

"But they knew who they were," Huw said.

"Yes," Myrddin said, "but as I had no choice, I didn't dwell on it." Myrddin paused. "Although, admittedly, I learned to fight almost before I could walk."

"And nobody seems to have any difficulty remembering who you are," Huw said.

Now Myrddin laughed. "Apparently not."

"When I began my search, I still called myself Huw ap Tomos, after my ... father," Huw said. "But as I approached Gwynedd, I met more people who knew you, or had heard of you. They mentioned one battle in particular, many years ago in the south, along the border with Mercia. You saved King Arthur's life that day."

Myrddin nodded at his son. "The king knighted me after that. It's his way to choose one man after each battle upon whom to confer the honor, and that day it was mine."

"I would like that for myself," Huw said. "Or, at least, I always saw myself serving in my lord's retinue. But now, I don't know what I'm meant to do; whom I'm meant to be or which lord I should serve."

"If you live honorably within yourself, it doesn't matter so much whom you serve," Myrddin said. This was Huw's real concern, and what had hovered over their conversation from the first.

Huw turned his head to look at Myrddin. "You believe that?"

Myrddin's eyes crinkled and his mouth twitched with sudden laughter, because Huw had caught him out. "Except in this case. If King Arthur loses this war, our country will fall to the Saxons. Modred cares only for himself and his own power—despite the fact that he himself is half-Welsh. He desires to completely subjugate my people—your people too—and all evidence suggests that he will settle for nothing less. Your lord, Cedric, knows this."

"Which is why he might be willing to ally himself with King Arthur," Huw said.

"Possibly," Myrddin said. "Cedric fears that were Arthur to die, or lose this war, it will embolden Modred. Cedric himself does not possess such a high standing with Modred that he might not lose everything too."

"Even though he and Modred are cousins through their fathers."

"Yes."

"So you're saying that it matters this time," Huw said. "You're saying that it has reached a point where I have to decide the greater loyalty."

"Yes, if Cedric sticks with Modred. You can't both be Welsh, and serve him. When Cedric himself freed me from Modred's grasp, however, he took a step towards shifting allegiance. It is also possible that Modred wanted me free, but wanted me freed covertly."

"Lord Cedric ap Aelfric has always dealt forthrightly with his men," Huw said, back to being a staunch supporter. "He is a good leader."

"I'll grant you that, but I must warn you, my son, that not everyone in this castle trusts your motives." Myrddin had deliberated with himself as to whether he should mention it, but the time seemed right.

"They fear I would betray King Arthur?" Huw said, eyes wide, a typical youth who still saw everything in black and white instead of realizing the world was mottled shades of grey.

"Think, Huw," Myrddin said. "This shouldn't surprise you. King Arthur has been betrayed by family, friends, and hidden foes more times than he can count. Is it any wonder some of his counselors would look askance at my newly claimed son who so conveniently rides to me from Brecon?"

"I see your point." Huw nodded, although Myrddin wasn't sure if he quite did.

"Just watch yourself," Myrddin said. "Better to keep silent and your eyes open."

"Yes, sir."

They were quiet a moment, and then Huw spoke again. "It was only chance, you know, that had me risk crossing the Conwy River and entering Eryri."

"Chance?" Myrddin said.

"In a tavern in Ruthin, I came upon a man who claimed to know you—or at least know the man whom the king knighted back in 525—but he told me you were dead. My heart fell. It seemed it was time to turn aside and return to Brecon."

"But you didn't," Myrddin said.

Huw shook his head. "Later in the evening, an argument developed between the man to whom I'd spoken and another. That man accused the first of being a liar and a traitor. The latter owed fealty to Arthur while the first had supported his brother, Cai, throughout his years of treachery." Huw glanced at Myrddin, his eyes thoughtful. "That was the tipping point. With my Lord Cedric on Anglesey, I was still free to search. I decided I wouldn't take the word of one man who did not hold with your allegiance."

"Praise God for that," Myrddin said.

"So what happens now?" Huw said.

"Cedric asked me to come to him at Brecon for the return of my horse. He's not ready to turn wholly away from Modred or turn to King Arthur. He intends, I think, to continue our discussion."

"Lord Cedric and his father once fought with Arthur." Huw tipped his chin upwards and stared at the rafters.

"They did," Myrddin said. "God willing, Cedric will again. I hope that once I've healed, you and I can journey together to convince him to honor that tradition."

* * * * *

Myrddin thought a single night at Garth Celyn should have been enough to heal him. Nell, on the other hand, was quite happy to have him more contained than usual. Bruised ribs could take weeks to mend. If they were right about what was coming for Wales and the king, Myrddin wasn't going to have the luxury of that much time. At least he was mobile, even if he looked and felt terrible.

The second evening back from Rhuddlan, Nell helped Myrddin hobble into the hall to share a meal with Ifan and Huw. The joy of Huw's very existence filled Myrddin's heart each time he said, *my son*, as if no man before him had ever had one. She could see it. It brought her nearly to tears every time—for Myrddin's sake and because her own heart lifted at the thought of one of her long-dead sons walking through the door. Huw was only two years older than her Llelo would have been.

They were halfway through the meal when instead of a beloved son, Deiniol pushed open the great doors and walked into the hall, an enormous grin on his face. Immediately behind him were Lord Gruffydd and his son, Owain. Cai, who'd been sitting at his place at the high table on Arthur's right, rose to his feet. "By God, I prayed you'd come!"

He headed around the table and in several long strides he and Owain met in the center of the hall, careless of who watched or what they thought of this development. As Owain and Gruffydd had been co-conspirators with Cai eight years before when they'd plotted to assassinate Arthur, it was understandable that some of Arthur's men might give him a rather less-than-effusive greeting.

Arthur, a smile on his lips that didn't reach his eyes, canted his head in greeting to Gruffydd, who strolled down the aisle between the tables until he reached the point opposite Arthur's seat.

"My king." Gruffydd bowed his head, although not perhaps as far as he could have.

"Gruffydd." Arthur gave his guest a similar, slight nod. The king gestured with his hand to the space beside him on his left, which Geraint had hastily vacated two seconds before. Normally, Bedwyr, Arthur's closest confident, sat next to him on the other side, but he'd not appeared for the meal. Could be, he didn't want to sit next to Cai, who'd taken his customary chair.

Then, inexplicably, Deiniol detached himself from Cai's side and strolled directly towards the four of them.

"What's he doing?" Myrddin said.

Nell put a hand on his arm, just in case he acted first and thought later. She didn't want Deiniol to insult her again, but didn't want Myrddin to cause a scene either. In his weakened condition, Myrddin was more vulnerable than she. Deiniol, for his part, remained polite. He stopped two feet from their table, put his heels together, and bowed to Nell.

"Madam," he said.

"Deiniol," she replied, aiming for graciousness, although she couldn't stop the twitch of a smile that lurked in the corner of her mouth at having to be polite to him. Perhaps humor might conquer Myrddin's loathing.

"So you didn't have a death wish after all," Myrddin said.

Nell elbowed him under the table, hitting a painful spot that left him gasping, and then smiled at Deiniol. "It was a great thing you did, bringing Gruffydd and Owain here. It must have been a dangerous journey."

Deiniol smiled, his eyes scanning Myrddin's bruised face. "It looks as if you had it rougher than I."

"It's been an eventful week in your absence," Myrddin said.

"Was the road difficult?" Nell said, still speaking as sweetly as she could.

"It was no trouble to serve my lord and bring new allies into his circle," Deiniol said.

Nell wasn't so sure about that.

"Does Modred know that Gruffydd's here?" Myrddin asked Deiniol.

He shrugged. "I doubt it. Gruffydd has always followed his own road." He lifted his chin, pointing at Huw. "Who's this?"

"My son," Myrddin said.

"Sir." Huw held a cup in his hand and motioned to Deiniol with it, the same amused expression she'd seen on his face at times when he talked to Myrddin, as if he couldn't quite believe he was actually in Garth Celyn, sitting beside his father.

Deiniol gave a laughing cough, saluted Myrddin with a slight motion of his hand, and moved on towards Cai, leaving the four companions staring after him.

Myrddin's eyes crinkled in the corners. Nell was glad to see his anger easing. Wearing a half smile, he sat back in his chair. "Three days ago, who would you have said were the three weakest links in Modred's control of Wales and the borderlands?"

"The lords Cedric, Edgar, and Gruffydd," Nell said.

"And now all three have come to call," Ifan said.

"Can he have all three, do you think?" Nell said. "Will they work with each other as well as with us?"

Myrddin made a 'maybe' movement with his head. "They've each fought Arthur in the past but they've also fought each other. It's Modred's response when he finds out that should give Gruffydd pause."

"If it's so dangerous, why is Gruffydd here?" Nell said.

"Because he's worried that Arthur will win," Ifan said. "He's afraid that if he waits too long to change sides, Arthur will no longer need him and when he wins, give his land to someone more deserving and loyal."

"Are we that close to victory?" Nell said.

"Gruffydd appears to think so," Myrddin said. "Perhaps the pressure from the Saxon barons Modred is trying to unite is greater than we thought."

9

"Excuse me—uh—Father—what are you doing?"

"I'm up," Myrddin said. "I am alive. I refuse to lie in that bed one hour longer."

"Are you really planning to ride today?"

Myrddin had entered the stables, thinking to get out of the hall and put aside his endless dreaming. It seemed that every time he closed his eyes, some new manifestation of his dream of Arthur's death swam before his eyes, each one different from the last.

"No." Snow had begun to fall, and at his son's words, Myrddin swung around to look behind him at the flakes floating in gentle wisps from the white sky. It had the look of continuing all day. "Up until right now, I'd forgotten Cadfarch wasn't here. I was going to brush him."

"I'm sorry," Huw said. "My lord will take good care of him."

"No doubt." Straw crunching underneath his feet, Myrddin walked to where Huw brushed his own horse and picked up a brush to work alongside his son.

"I'm surprised Nell let you get up."

"She's seeing to a birth," Myrddin said. "She doesn't know."

"Is she your woman, like everyone says?" Huw carefully combed his horse's mane rather than looking at Myrddin.

"I don't know that she'd characterize herself that way," Myrddin said. "To her mind, she's nobody's woman but her own. At the same time, between you and me—and the rest of the garrison—no man should think otherwise."

Huw nodded. "I've spoken to Ifan of your injuries. When you said that they were at Modred's behest, I hadn't realized that he was actually *present* when his guards administered them."

"Yes." Myrddin ran his hand down the horse's legs, feeling his sturdy hocks for damage. "Modred does as he pleases."

"My lord!"

The call shattered the peace and in four strides Myrddin and Huw arrived at the entrance to the stables to look out on a small company of men just coming through the gate. Gareth led them, the white plume on his helmet fading into the snowy landscape. The man beside him wore the garments of a member of the clergy, although he'd drawn up his hood to protect himself from the weather so Myrddin couldn't see his face. *Surely that's not one of Gareth's cousins?*

But then the priest turned to hand his horse's reins to Adda and Myrddin saw the face beneath the covering hood. The man was Anian, the Bishop of St. Asaph, who'd been party to the excommunication of King Arthur at Rhuddlan Castle.

"What's he doing here?" Myrddin said.

"Joining the fold, it seems." Huw turned back to his horse. As he did so, he asked casually—although the question was anything but casual. "You distrust him?"

"I trust very few men," Myrddin said.

"Not Deiniol, certainly," Huw said. "Nell told me of your quarrels."

"It's more than a quarrel," Myrddin said, "for all that we've spoken no more than three sentences to each other in twenty years."

"And Cai?" Huw said. "You loathe him."

"That goes without saying," Myrddin said. "These men are known traitors to King Arthur. It's the ones who hide behind their loyalty while pocketing coins from Modred that concern me. Of them, there may be none or many, even here."

Huw picked up the brush for currying his horse and plucked at the hairs in it.

Myrddin watched him, waiting for the question he knew was coming.

"And me? Do you trust me?"

If Myrddin could have told Huw without humiliating him that he was transparent, he would have. As it was, he clapped his son on the shoulder. "I trust you. When I told you earlier that some here didn't, I did not mean me."

"What if my lord really did send me to find you in order to act as his spy among your people?" Huw said.

"Did he?"

"No," Huw said, indignant, despite the fact that he'd been the first to pose the question.

"Lord Cedric undoubtedly hoped that you would serve him in that capacity anyway." Myrddin said, and at Huw's stuttered protest held up a hand to stop him speaking. "Imagine you are a lord of Mercia and one of your men, one of the younger squires, tells you that his real father is someone other than the staunch companion of your youth. He's a Welshman you've never met. The boy asks to seek this new father out. You know that the boy's mother is Welsh.

You understand how his two allegiances could pull him apart, regardless of how noble you believe him to be."

"So you send him north." Huw nodded. "And hope that he finds his father and that through that relationship, whether or not the boy wishes it, you discover something you didn't know about the King Arthur's plans."

"It is a sensible approach," Myrddin said. "Logical too. It's not even deceitful."

"If the boy comes home empty-handed, he has information about the disposition of Arthur's men and the interior of Wales you hadn't known before." Huw paused. "I would have been eager to tell Lord Cedric all I'd learned."

"It is the perfect plan," Myrddin said. "Cedric risks only you, who have requested this mission. At best, he gains knowledge; at worst, he loses a good squire."

"At worst." Huw studied his boots.

"When I met Cedric," Myrddin moved closer to Huw and took the brush so Huw would look at him, "he was surprised at first. But he recognized my name, and because of that, he freed me from Modred's clutches."

"So I would find you," Huw said. "So I would spy for him."

Myrddin shook his head. "Cedric's position in Wales is unstable. You cannot blame him for using whatever weapons come to hand, especially if he can wield them at so little cost to himself."

This was too much for Huw. The knowledge that he'd been used by his lord stuck in his throat and he couldn't swallow it. He turned to Myrddin and stepped close, his face right in his father's. He wasn't angry as much as fierce. "Would you ever do that to me?"

"I would tell you," Myrddin said, "and make you a willing party to my plans. I promise you that."

Huw shot Myrddin an unreadable look from those pale eyes, nodded, and stepped away, back to his horse. Myrddin didn't know if Huw was truly reassured or if he no longer knew what to believe.

"But I am your father," Myrddin added. "In his present, precarious state, Cedric doesn't have time for niceties. Don't be too hard on him."

Huw didn't answer. Instead, he pawed through the saddle bags that rested on a hook in his horse's stall. He took out a wad of old cloth that looked like nothing more than a bandage yet to be used on an injured man. He unfolded it and held his hand out to Myrddin. A heavy gold cross on a thick chain lay in Huw's palm. At the sight of it, Myrddin stepped closer, his breath catching in his throat.

"Christ's bones, Huw, I've not seen that cross ..." Myrddin's voice died as he realized where he'd last seen it.

"Since you gave it to my mother," Huw said. "I know."

Myrddin reached out a finger and touched it, feeling the smooth metal and remembering when he'd given it to her. The cross had weighed on his neck, dangling between them as Myrddin had made love to her. He'd placed it around her neck instead. In his mind's eye, he saw it settle between her breasts and warm there.

He'd spent the night in her bed; then left in the early hours of the morning at the command of his king. At the time, he'd meant for Tegwan to keep it. Myrddin had been nineteen years old, in love and a romantic. It seemed appropriate to give her the one thing of value that he possessed, barring his sword.

"It was my mother's. I've always assumed that her father gave it to her, although it has crossed my mind that she could have gotten it from mine." He looked into Huw's face. "It's yours, now."

"No." Huw shook his head. "You're still young enough to marry. Although my mother cherished it, I have many things from her, including sixteen years of memories. If you want to give it away again, give it to Nell." He pushed his hand towards Myrddin and Myrddin didn't resist him. He lifted the cross from Huw's palm by its chain, caressing the smooth links.

"Thank you." Myrddin forced the words past the thickening in his throat. "My nurse gave this to me when I was twelve, believing that I should have something of my mother. She had kept it hidden all those years, knowing that if Madoc found it, he could claim it for himself as payment for giving me house room until I became a man." Myrddin slipped the chain over his head and tucked the cross under his shirt. It was an unfamiliar weight against his breastbone, but a comforting one.

"May it protect you wherever you go," Huw said, "as it has me."

* * * * *

"I dreamed last night." Nell stood in the doorway of their room, gazing down on Myrddin who lay spread-eagled on his pallet. Huw remained in the hall where he would spend the night amongst the other squires and men-at-arms who were arriving in increasing numbers with their lords, in preparation for the meeting of the Welsh High Council.

Nell had asked Huw if he would prefer to share their room even though Myrddin no longer needed watching over.

The appalled look on his face had prompted laughter from Nell. Myrddin and Nell had become more than friends, but what exactly they were to each other, Nell wasn't quite sure. The rest of the castle assumed they knew, however, and if that meant she could continue to stay with him, then that was fine by her. Like the breeches she'd worn to Rhuddlan, the idea was freeing.

"I dream every night," he said.

"Will you tell me about them?" Nell would have asked him about the dreams days ago, but he'd been ill and she almost hadn't wanted to share them with him because once she did, they'd both be laid bare. While they'd admitted the truth to each other, what that truth entailed, and what they were going to do about it, wasn't at all clear.

"Do I have a choice?" Myrddin said, and then smiled, taking the sting out of his words. He gestured to Nell with one hand. She entered the room and closed the door behind her; then walked to the pallet on which Myrddin lay and knelt on the end of it. Myrddin pushed himself upright and braced his back against the wall. "All right." He scrubbed at his face with both hands. "Talk to me."

"My dreams have changed."

"Have they?" he said. "How?"

"Except for that first instance, I've always fought as you when I dream. But since before you went to Rhuddlan, it's been different. Sometimes you're not even there. Last night, more men filled the clearing than before, and there were no archers. In fact—" she paused, trying to think how to say this, "—although you were there, you didn't die."

"Really." Myrddin dropped his hands to his lap. "And that's different?"

"Yes, of course."

"Certainly, I have no interest in dying just yet." They sat silent for a moment, before Myrddin continued, "I don't just want to save King Arthur because I want to save Wales—I have this odd idea that if I save him, I save myself."

"There's nothing wrong with not wanting to die by a Saxon's sword," Nell said.

"In my dream last night, I didn't have Cadfarch," Myrddin said. "That might be the first time. And since just before I met you, I've not worn a mustache."

Nell's eyes widened. "And that's my fault! But I didn't know!"

"No," Myrddin said. "Only because I didn't tell you, and yet ..."

"Does that mean that actions we take in the real world change our dreams, which in turn indicates a new course in the future?" Nell said. "That we're making progress?"

"What is progress?" Myrddin said. "We have no idea if everything we're doing right now is exactly what we need to do to ensure that King Arthur dies on December 11th. There's no reason to think otherwise."

"Except that if King Arthur's death is inevitable, why dream?"

Myrddin snorted under his breath. "You're assuming these dreams don't come from the devil."

"Oh, yes," Nell said. "I thought it at first, of course. I told my father of the vision the first time I had it. I ran home, screaming of the battle I'd witnessed and the dead men. Once past the clearing, the world reverted to what it had been. But when my father searched, he found nothing by the river. He was afraid for me, then."

"Did you ever tell a priest?"

"Did you?"

Myrddin gave a sharp laugh. "No."

"So what *did* you do?" Nell said. "Up until now, I mean."

"I came to serve the king as soon as I was able," Myrddin said. "But otherwise, I ignored the dreams. I drank."

"You drank." Nell strove to keep her voice even. "And what good was that supposed to do?"

"Goddamn it! I don't know!" Myrddin said. "Who am I to change the world? Who am I to have these visions?"

Nell bit her lip as she looked at him, realizing she'd pressed too hard. "You're Myrddin. Why not you?"

"What about you, then?" Myrddin said, still angry. "You were doing no more than I. Less, in fact. You were leaving Wales."

Nell looked down at her hands folded in her lap, and then back up at Myrddin. "No, I wasn't."

"That's what you told me."

"I lied." Nell forced herself not to look away from Myrddin's face.

"You lied." He mimicked the flatness in her tone.

Nell nodded. "I was going to Rhuddlan, as I said, but my intent was to enter the castle."

"For what purpose?" Myrddin said. "As a spy?"

"Not exactly." Nell shrugged. She glanced away, unable to maintain eye contact. Now that it came to it, perhaps he'd find the truth far worse than his basest suspicions. She felt his gaze on her and still she wouldn't look at him. "I wasn't a nun anymore, you know."

"Christ!" Myrddin leaned forward to grab her chin. "You weren't going there as a spy! You were going as—as a—as a whore!"

There it was, the truth at last. Nell pulled away, pummeled by Myrddin's horrified stare. She shrugged again. "It was an idea."

"My God! What were you thinking?"

"I'll tell you what I was thinking!" She looked up, her anger flaring. "The solution to our problems certainly wasn't to drink myself into a stupor every night. I was going to get close to Modred! And kill him if I could! It might even have been easy—just a knife in the back after I refilled his goblet. I might not even have had to sell myself to do it."

Myrddin's mouth was open as he stared her.

Nell gritted her teeth, determined to tell him everything. "My sisters had already suffered worse at the hands of Wulfere's soldiers. It was the least I could do! And it was the only thing I could think of that *I* could do to change the future."

Myrddin leaned forward and gripped her arms. "You must have realized that Modred's men would have killed you immediately afterwards."

"Of course."

"*Christ!*" Myrddin blasphemed again. "That was the stupidest idea I've ever heard!" He shook her. Once. While she glared at him, trying to hang on to her anger even though tears pricked at her eyes. She opened her mouth to speak but then he put one finger to her lips to stop her, his voice softening. "And the bravest."

With that, she couldn't constrain the tears. They spilled out the corners of her eyes and down her cheeks. Myrddin made a 'tsk' noise from between his teeth and pulled her to him. Nell wrapped her arms around his waist and sobbed into his chest.

"Sweet Mary, mother of God, that you would think that was your only choice," Myrddin said. "You would have died."

"That was, in part, the point," Nell said. "By then I would have done anything. Anything to stop the dreams. Anything to stop King Arthur from meeting Edgar by the Cam River."

"Thank God I found you. I wish I'd done so long ago."

"You didn't know of me," she said. "Better that I'd tried to find you. Silly of me not to think of it; I don't know why I didn't."

"I'll be damned if I'll ever bow to a Saxon lord again!"

The fierce tones of Lord Gruffydd carried loudly through the wall. Nell froze in Myrddin's arms. As his words sank in, they eased back from each other. Nell wished she could see right through the wall to the other side.

"We've had little choice—" another voice said.

"He's talking to Cai," Nell said.

"You have had a choice!" Gruffydd hammered at him. "You would rather see Wales fall under the Saxon boot than lose an acre of what you possess? Even if Modred wins this war, you have no guarantee he will confirm you as Lord of Gwynedd. Look what has happened to Edgar of Wigmore!" Gruffydd sounded so much like Arthur, it was as if he'd become a different person.

"That's just one instance—"

Gruffydd cut off Cai again. "One instance that we are to take as an example for all of us! If he can do this to his loyal cousin, the man who stood by him through every war this century, he can do it to any of us."

"You've stood at Modred's side many times," Cai said, still defiant and forceful. "Why not now? Why not this time?"

"Because he betrayed me with my wife!"

The silence in both rooms was deafening. Gruffydd had married a much younger woman after the death of Owain's mother. His confession had Nell holding her breath, one hand clenching and unclenching around Myrddin's arm. Surely they must realize that the walls had ears?

Finally, Cai spoke again. "How do you know?"

"She told me that he'd asked for her. When I confronted him, he laughed. He admitted he'd taken her." Now, Gruffydd lowered his voice, forcing Nell to lean in to hear the conversation better. She pressed her ear to the wall that separated the two rooms. "He thinks he controls me."

"Admittedly, Modred consorts with many women," Cai said. "It is well known."

"But never *my* woman," Gruffydd said.

"I can see that you are confirmed in your opinion." Cai returned to his normal speaking voice. "I will not try to change it."

"And you?" Gruffydd said. "You stand beside your brother for all to see, yet you mean to tell me that you spy for Modred?"

"I do not spy." There was a distinct *clunk* against the wall. Nell imagined Cai had pressed Gruffydd to it and she shrank back, as if Cai might be able to sense her through the wall. Ten heartbeats passed and then feet retreated across the floor. A door to the hall slammed.

"I see," Gruffydd said, presumably to himself.

"I don't see. Are we to understand that Cai's faithfulness is a front? A sham to gain power and land?" Nell turned to Myrddin, whose jaw was set in a more grim line than she'd ever seen it.

"Yes. That is precisely what we must understand. It is as it has always been. I just don't know what to do about it."

"You could tell King Arthur."

"Just like I can tell him about our dreams? He would not believe me, *could* not believe me without proof."

"Then Bedwyr or Geraint," she said.

Myrddin shook his head. "Not yet. We still have time."

"We hope we still have time," she said.

The Lion of Wales series continues with the third
novella in the series:
Of Men and Dragons

Made in the USA
Middletown, DE
06 August 2015